Broken Dreams

Dawn Pendleton

*Pearl —
May all your
dreams be unbroken!

Dawn
Pendleton*

Broken Dreams

Dawn Pendleton

© 2013 Dawn Pendleton
http://www.dawnpendleton.com

Any unauthorized reprint or use of this material is prohibited. No part of this book may be reproduced or transmitted in any form without express written permission from the author/publisher.

This is a work of fiction. Names, characters, places and events are the product of the author's imagination and any resemblance to any persons, living or dead, business establishments, events, or locales is entirely coincidental.

Dedication

This book is dedicated to my little sister, who turns sixteen this year and who shares my immense love of reading and writing. Someday, our names will be side-by-side on a publication.

Chapter One

Rainey

The plane landed on the runway without a single hiccup. Of course, my hands gripped the armrests like a lifeline and I couldn't make myself let go until the flight attendant came to check on me long after everyone else was off the plane. My hands shook until I walked through the walkway into the airport; my feet were finally on solid ground.

That morning, I woke up in my own bed in Los Angeles, took a taxi to LAX, popped a Valium, and boarded my plane. I was lucky enough to find a nonstop flight to Boston, but it had been difficult. I wasn't much of a flier. The puddle-jumper plane that guided me from Boston to Portland, Maine, was, in my opinion, not even equipped to fly. But the staff assured me it was. On several occasions. So I sat perfectly still for the entire half-hour flight, hands glued to the armrests. The Valium had long ago worn off, which meant I wasn't as relaxed as I wanted to be.

It wasn't that I hated flying. I simply despised flying so much that I would feel safer jumping out of the damn airplane than riding inside it. But it landed. *Thank God.* I made my way through the terminal and toward baggage claim. My mother claimed she would pick me up, but I wasn't about to hold my breath. She was the most unreliable woman I'd ever met in my life, and that included my flighty aunt, Brittney.

I rounded the corner to baggage claim and found my mother's void eyes staring at me. She waited for me to approach and made no effort to hug me. I nodded to her. She resented me for going to live with my aunt. It wasn't a decision I'd made lightly, but it still burned that she didn't respect my decision. Of course, there were things about my life she didn't know, so I couldn't blame her too much. I'd hidden my *real* life from so many people.

I'd only been away from Maine for a week. After spending three weeks in my hometown of Casper, Maine, helping my best friend, Mallory, deal with the death of her father, I'd made the final decision to move back home. Mallory needed support through her grief, and even though she had her boyfriend, Luke, I felt like I should move back, at least for the summer.

She was my reasoning for moving home, but the truth was so much more complex. But I promised her I would move home for the summer, and I meant to keep my promise. When I'd flown to LA last week, Mallory dropped me at the airport, demanding I not change my mind.

"There's no way I'm letting you leave me here all summer to handle Baker," she protested when I joked about not coming back.

Baker was just another complication of my life. He took me to my high school prom and was a perfect gentleman, which led me to giving him my virginity at the age of eighteen. That summer, though, his best friend and mine broke up. The breakdown of Luke and Mallory's relationship had spurred me to ignore anyone who affiliated with Luke. And that included Baker. It was too bad, too, since I'd had a crush on him for nearly all four years of high school. But when couples break up, everyone around them must choose sides.

"I'll come back, Mal. It's only a week so I can figure out what I'm going to ship here and what I'm having Aunt Britt toss out," I reassured my best friend.

Mallory was fragile and I knew she was worried about me. Even though I explained how little chance there was of a relapse, she still worried. It made sense. Her father died of cancer just two weeks ago. So, finding out her best friend had leukemia was a shock.

I didn't want to tell her. Hell, I didn't even want to admit it to myself. But she'd begged and pleaded until I confessed. It pissed her off that Gabby, our other best friend, knew before she did. Then again, Gabby knew before anyone. She was the very first person I told two-and-a-half years ago. Plus, Mallory had been dealing with her father's cancer; she didn't need to worry about mine. I was in remission. There was no reason to think it would come back, either. I'd been cancer free for five whole months. It didn't seem like a long time, but every other time the doctors said the leukemia was in remission, it came back within six weeks. Five months was practically a lifetime.

"Did you eat on the plane?" my mother asked. I gulped down my immediate nausea.

"No, but I'm not all that hungry. We can just go home," I suggested. We made our way out of the airport once I grabbed my extra-large duffel bag. Aunt Britt was going to mail larger packages of my things.

She didn't speak while she drove. Casper was an hour away from the airport and the silence gave me some time to truly think about being back in my hometown. I didn't hate the town, or anyone in it. My reasons for leaving had been the pursuit of an escape from my mother. The reason I stayed in the city, however, was that I fell in love with LA.

There was always something going on in Southern California, whether it was a movie production or premiere, or even just a party at one of the frats at UCLA. It was a busy place and I never sat home on a weekend debating whether I should hit up the local pizza place or do something out of town like I did during high school in Casper.

LA was the land of dreams, and although mine probably weren't going to come true, I loved living there. But the more I watched the people around me achieve their dreams, the more I realized I would never be able to stay there forever. Perhaps my aunt was right and I should consider moving back to Casper permanently. It wasn't something I was ready to decide, though. Spending the summer in the small town would hopefully steer me in the right direction. Until then, I just wanted to enjoy myself.

My mother didn't expect me to stay home during my vacation, which meant I needed to make plans, since she would likely be heavily sedated on Xanax and tequila by dinnertime. She was predictable as ever. Halfway through the hour-long drive, she pulled over, feigned a headache, and asked me to drive. She popped a few pills and took a swig off the to-go mug she had with her. I didn't bother asking her what was inside the mug. I already knew.

I supposed I should be grateful for the fact that she remained sober until I got in. I wasn't, though. I resented her. I had spent my high school years taking care of her, instead of her taking care of me. She always guilted me into staying home and throwing a party instead of going out with my friends. She was the ultimate party mom and all my friends loved her. But they never saw behind the scenes. Well, Mallory and Gabby did, but they were the only ones. All my other girlfriends had been blissfully unaware of the turmoil I faced every day at home.

I tried not to think about the past as I pulled the mini-van back onto the highway. Mom's head was already tilted against the glass, her eyes closed and a soft snore escaping her nose. I sighed.

It was going to be an emotional summer. Her constant inebriation was part of the reason I left, but it was my extended stay at Cedars Sinai hospital that convinced me to remain in LA. Well, more like my aunt convinced me to stay based on my hospital visit. Aunt Britt was the one who explained that I needed to be cared for, not to care for someone else. Mom wasn't going to be able to give me the kind of care I needed after my hospital stay.

I found out about my leukemia two short weeks after my father was killed in a car accident. I'd only been in LA for a month and had just started my classes at UCLA. As much as I wanted to spend months grieving, the knowledge of my cancer pushed me to *live*. It was, as Aunt Britt pointed out, exactly what my dad would have wanted.

Mom took his death the hardest, although I was hardly in a good place. She called me every ten minutes for two weeks after I moved back to LA, professing her love for him and questioning why God would do this to her. As much as I tried to understand, I resented her for expecting me to be there for her when she couldn't be there for me. Eventually, I stopped trying to comfort her over the phone from LA and she stopped calling. I went an entire year before I came home to visit and she and I were awkward in our relationship. But, I made the effort. For Daddy.

When I pulled down Main Street in Casper, I smiled. Feelings of contentment and *coming home* filled me. Whether I liked LA or not, this was home for me. This was where I belonged. I passed the only full-service gas station in town, the post office, and a newly renovated book store. The sidewalks were filled with people.

As a tourist town, people came from all over the country to visit Casper. The shops and epic coastline drew them in, but what kept them coming back was the feeling of community and the bubbly personalities most residents had. The ocean was a short trip down the peninsula, where the lighthouse glowed late at night.

I looked forward to heading to the beach while I was here. California boasted beautiful beaches, but nothing beat the beaches in Maine. The sand was rugged, a testament to the number of storms the state got. Hurricane season usually left a small mark, but winter storms tore the coast of Maine up. I even missed the snow while I was in LA.

The drive through Casper was short, given its size. In a matter of minutes, I was out of the center of town and turning onto the road that led to my mother's house. It hardly qualified as a house, though. The mobile home was set back from the road on a tiny piece of land. It was the only thing Dad let her keep when they divorced.

Theirs was a relationship that left me baffled. After their divorce, they got back together several times, though they didn't marry again. The fact that they spent two years apart, though, meant that I had step-siblings. Not that I saw them often. Dallas was twenty-four and traveled for his job. I secretly coveted his photographer's lifestyle. Not only was he talented with a lens, but he also went from place to place and lived as a nomad. He never stayed in the same place longer than a few months. He'd visited me in LA twice during the last three years; he was one of the few people who knew about my illness. As far as I knew, he didn't have any plans to come to Maine, though. I didn't blame him.

Ember was seventeen and would be graduating high school in a few weeks. She was smart, sassy, and gorgeous. At seventeen, she had more grace and style than most women had in a lifetime. Of course, her mother was a model, which probably contributed to her fashion sense. She only lived a few towns away from Casper, so I would be able to go to her graduation, just as I promised her I would.

Our family was split up in a chaotic way. Dallas and I shared a mother, but had different fathers. We grew up in the same house until he was sixteen. His father offered him an internship at his photography firm in Virginia, and he'd spent the summer there. He refused to come back to Casper after that, choosing instead to finish his high school degree in Virginia.

After he graduated, he began his roaming tendencies, refusing to settle down. He didn't want to end up like so many of the people in Casper who never left, never got to see the world. I'd done the same thing, in a sense. Ember and I had different mothers, lucky her. She was only fifteen when Dad died, and it had been a rough time for her. I hadn't been able to be there for her like I wanted, as I was dealing with my own issues, but I kept in close contact with her through the years. She even flew out to see me last summer.

Ember's birth had been a severe hiccup in my parent's relationship, and had ultimately caused their divorce. But Dad's infidelity brought me a little sister, one I adored. She was going places, and with Dad gone, I felt it my responsibility to make sure she did. Her mother, Victoria, was always pleasant whenever Ember invited me over when we were younger, and she made me feel right at home in their house.

I pulled into the driveway of Mom's place and parked. I looked over at her slumped form and shook my head in disgust. The woman couldn't even stay sober for my homecoming. I left her there in the passenger seat, grabbed my bag, and made my way into the house. My room was the smallest of three and when I opened up the bedroom door, it was still a shock to see that all traces of my youth were washed away. The room was made up as a guest room without any of my adolescent boy band posters or my belongings, and although I had time to adjust to the fact that my mother erased a piece of me, it still stung.

The quotes from poems and my favorite books I'd written on the walls had been painted over with a brilliantly white paint. Even the desk had been painted to cover all the phone numbers I wrote on it in permanent marker. I swallowed the lump in my throat. When I'd come home last Christmas, everything had been painted over. I wasn't sure how I felt about everything being wiped away.

It was as if she had deleted a piece of my past. I made my way to the painted desk and yanked open the top drawer. I breathed a sigh of relief. All of my photos were neatly stacked inside. At least she hadn't erased me completely. I closed the drawer, not yet wanting to go down memory lane.

I tossed my bag onto the bed and pulled the door closed behind me as I went to get Mom out of the van. I walked passed Dallas's bedroom and the door was partially open. I pushed it and stood there, dumbfounded. I hadn't noticed his room when I'd been home two weeks ago.

Whereas my room had been turned into a guest room, Dallas's bedroom had become a shrine. Covering the walls were photos he'd taken, photos of him taking photos, and copies of the awards he'd won in the last few years. All were framed and hung proudly. I stared at the walls, knowing how much Dallas would hate it. She did it in tribute, I was sure, but if he saw it, he'd rip each photo, each award from the walls and declare he didn't want anyone to put him up on a pedestal like that.

But Dallas hadn't been to Casper in a long time. I tried to remember if I'd come into his room last Christmas. I didn't think I did, as I would have remembered what she'd done. I stepped out of the room, vaguely aware that it smelled like Dallas. She must know what cologne he wore. I closed the door and never wanted to open it again, hating her for loving him more than me. But I managed a deep breath as I went back outside to help her into bed.

It was going to be a long summer.

Chapter Two

Baker

Owning a bar was a pain in the ass.

Aside from the fact that I had to figure out the payroll and QuickBooks and all sorts of clerical crap like that, I had to work at least fifty hours a week, usually more. Until Memorial Day, we were only open Thursday and Friday nights and all day Saturday and Sunday. But it wasn't like those were the only days I worked.

Payroll went through on Mondays and then on Tuesdays we got our liquor shipments, with any beer and keg order coming in on Wednesday. And for the first six months, I tried to do it all myself. I don't remember sleeping at all during those first six months.

But the summer season was coming and I decided to bite the bullet and hire a bar manager. It was an expense I didn't really have the money for, but I was also running myself ragged trying to do everything alone. Hiring Jimmy had been a smart choice, but a difficult one. His salary raised my payroll and I wasn't sure we would make it. I needed to make more money.

I could always pick up more shifts with JP Construction, the company Luke worked for. Luke was my best friend and he was always throwing my name at JP for extra work. I appreciated it, but sometimes it felt like charity. So I tried not to work for JP too much. Once or twice a week helped keep me afloat. It also meant I didn't have to cut a paycheck for myself yet.

Summer was just around the corner, though, which meant The Landing would be busy as hell. After the renovations I made last fall, I expected a much larger crowd this season. The bar and restaurant literally sat on a dock in the water. It wasn't the ocean, but an inlet that led to the ocean and so the water was brackish but the tides came and went like they did at the coast. The deck had been completely redone and expanded so our capacity limit had increased. There was also an outside bar for those hot summer nights when being cooped up inside a bar wasn't as much fun as dancing the night away under the stars.

Inside, I made the bar bigger and the band area now boasted a step-down dance floor and area seating. The band area was also somewhat separate from the bar so that patrons who wanted to hear the music but not necessarily dance could sit at the bar top or choose from several pub tables. It all looked very different and so far, no one had complained.

The renovations tied up a lot of money, though. So I kept a skeleton crew through the winter and now I had to hire more employees, before we really got busy to make sure everyone was trained. More payroll. *Fuck.*

I don't know what made me think I was qualified to run a bar, other than the fact that I loved to drink. Beer, whiskey, rum, tequila; I loved them all. And now that I owned the place, I hardly ever drank. So much for a frivolous youth. No denying it now; I was an adult. It sucked to grow up.

Not drinking had its perks, though. I was continuously amused by patrons who went overboard and then tried to dance. Or sing. Or speak at all. Regardless of whether they were seasoned veterans or the just-turned-twenty-one partiers, drunk people were freaking hilarious. On Friday nights, the drunk girls would shake their asses for the drunk guys, and I couldn't help but notice that they couldn't dance. I never noticed that when I was the drunken one. Their bodies all convulsed, not even in unison with the beat. It was comical.

I hooked up two kegs to the bar tap and then went to unload the bottles in crates from this morning's delivery. Even though we didn't have stellar sales last weekend, I hoped this weekend would be better. I hired a band for Friday and Saturday night, spending more money I didn't really have, but I didn't have much choice, either. Bands drew in larger crowds. Larger crowds meant more money in my pocket. Or, well, in the pockets of the bar. Either way, it was win-win.

Once all my inventory was recorded and put away, I went into the beyond-tiny office behind the bar. My desk took up most of the space, with a small shelf in the corner filling up the rest. Papers flooded my desk and I groaned in anticipation. It would be a long afternoon.

Several hours later, I looked up and realized Jimmy would be arriving for his shift anytime now. I stretched and yawned.

"Tired, boss?" Jimmy said from the doorway.

"Not a chance. You ready for work tonight?"

"Mostly. I just have to cut up some fruit and make sure the kegs are all full," he replied.

"I took care of the kegs. Your coolers are all fully stocked, too. You work on fruit," I said with a grin. Jimmy *hated* cutting fruit, which was exactly why I left it for him.

"Great," he said in a sarcastic tone. "Are you going to take care of the next schedule, or do you want me to?"

I couldn't hide my surprise. "You want to do the schedule?"

"Well, yeah. I figured it's part of my job as bar manager now."

"Yes. Take care of it." I all but threw the scheduling paperwork at him. He caught it with a grimace and then shook his head.

"What sort of schedule do you work?" He wasn't being insubordinate; most local owners hardly worked any hours in their establishments at all.

"I'll bounce on Friday and Saturday nights, but other than that, keep me open and I'll fill in where necessary." I stood and stretched again, avoiding another yawn.

"Got it. Will you be here tonight?"

"I'll be here around six. For now, I'm going to take care of a few things," I said. "Feel free to use my office for doing the schedule. Open up at four," I instructed.

He nodded and we looked ridiculous as we moved around each other in the small space as I made my way out. I nodded to him and then took off. I jumped in my truck and rolled my shoulders. I needed to relax. I pulled out my cell as I turned the ignition. My truck roared to life, as did the stereo. I muted the volume and dialed Luke.

"Hey, Baker, what's up?" he answered.

"I've got a few hours to kill before I go back to the bar. You done with work?"

"Yeah, just got done. If we're going out, I need to shower. What did you have in mind?" he asked.

"I was thinking about playing some basketball," I told him.

"Sounds good. I'll meet you at the court in fifteen?"

"Sure."

I pressed the red button on my phone and tossed it in the cup holder. Basketball would be the perfect detox for this already hellish week. I knew Luke could use the time, too.

I drove to the basketball courts and parked in the parking lot of The Wharf. It was the nearest parking lot. The Wharf was a fresh seafood takeout place on the peninsula. It was right on the water with scenic views of the coast. Everyone loved it. The food was great, but most of the tourists went there for the view. Locals ate there because you could eat a lobster that had been caught that day.

I grabbed my ball and shoes out of the backseat and walked across the street to the courts. Luke wasn't there yet, so I sat on a bench and changed my shoes. My work shoes were the black, slip-resistant, uncomfortable, crappy shoes the state required, but my basketball sneakers were made to fit my feet. Sleek black-and-white Nikes with the signature checkmark on the side. I pulled the laces tight and tied them. I was proud of my shoes. They were one of the few things I had that were new.

My truck was a '94 and most of my clothes were old or cheap. I lived on a limited salary, though. So when I spent a hundred bucks on basketball shoes, I made sure they got the respect they deserved. Luke walked up as I finished tying. He sat on the bench beside me and changed his shoes.

"How's Mallory?" I asked. Her father died a few weeks ago and I knew she wasn't quite back to normal.

"Surprisingly good. She's been going to a therapist in Portland, and she's excited for Rainey to come back," he replied. He gave me a look and lifted an eyebrow at me suggestively.

I laughed. "Rainey has made it clear that anything we have is only for the summer. She's not moving back permanently. And that's perfect for me. A summer fling is just what the doctor ordered."

Luke shook his head, then stood and grabbed the ball off the bench. He dribbled down the court and I chased after him, determined to win this game. But my heart wasn't in it.

I thought about Rainey and all she'd been through in the past, even recently. She was a tough woman, I had to give her that. When she showed up for Joe, Mallory's dad, to say I was surprised was an understatement.

The bar was filling up; business was going to be good. It was Friday night and the band was blaring. I was checking IDs at the door. Nothing safer than being in charge of who got in my bar. It was my insurance so there were no underage kids inside.

A group of women approached and I stamped each of their hands after checking their ages. They wandered inside, giggling and whispering as they passed me. I laughed at their antics but kept my mind on the job. When a blonde woman approached by herself, I straightened up. She gave me a shy smile as a she walked up and looked at me expectantly.

I couldn't shake the feeling I knew her, but I couldn't place her. She was familiar but gorgeous; I was certain if I actually knew her, I wouldn't have forgotten her. Then I looked into her bright green eyes. They were striking and the realization of who she was hit me like a punch in the gut.

"Rainey?" I asked.

"Hey, Baker," she said. Her smile widened.

"You – wow, you look... Damn, girl! You sure have changed," I said. And as if I hadn't made enough of a fool of myself, I kept speaking. "You used to be so big!"

My eyes widened as soon as the words were out of my mouth. I hadn't meant to say that. Yes, she lost a lot of weight, but her weight never bothered me before. In fact, she looked too skinny now. She wasn't the same curvy girl I remembered.

"Nice, Baker. Way to welcome me back," she laughed and shrugged past me into the bar.

I turned to watch her make her way to the table Mallory and Gabby were already seated at. I felt like such a douche.

That night had been one to remember. Luke broke up with his girlfriend for Mallory that night, and I'd driven Rainey home. Since then, we'd kind of been together, but it wasn't until she left to settle her affairs in LA for the summer that I realized how much fun we were going to have in the coming weeks. I planned to treat her right, not only because I liked her, but also to make up for being an ass that first night.

We'd texted back and forth nearly the whole time she was back in LA. She was witty and sarcastic, just like I remembered. The only thing that had changed about her, it seemed, was her weight. I'd never believed she was fat, but I knew she'd been picked on a lot during high school for her size. It pissed me off but Rainey took it with class and usually delivered a reply to her tormentors that cut them down in a way that led them to leave her alone.

It was amazing to watch her in action. She never raised her voice or got emotional, either. She kept a calm demeanor, which I think made her more frightening. She was a force to be reckoned with.

I smiled as I stole the ball away from Luke. Best friend or not, I could still whoop his ass at basketball. He chased after me down the court but never had a chance. I tossed the ball and it swished into the net. I cheered my success and Luke grumbled something about me being a cheater. I let it go and grinned wider.

"Jealousy will get you nowhere, my friend," I said. It was so much fun to taunt him. He gave me the evil eye.

We played for nearly an hour before he gave up the fight.

"Let's call it a day," he suggested. He looked forlorn and depressed. I laughed at his lack of enthusiasm.

"Sure thing, Luke. What's on the agenda tonight?" I asked, wondering if he and Mallory would come to the bar.

Luke had sworn off drinking a while, afraid he was going to turn into his alcoholic father. I knew he would be fine, especially with Mallory to keep him in check. But he was still a little gun shy about drinking these days.

"Mal and I will probably come have dinner at the bar. If it stays nice like this, she said she wanted to eat outside on the deck."

"Great. I've got to head home and shower. I'll see you guys there," I said as I changed out of my basketball shoes and back into my work shoes. I bumped his knuckles with mine and made my way to my truck. As I tossed my bag in the passenger seat, I looked back at the court where Luke was dribbling down the court. He did it every time we played.

Luke wasn't out of shape by any means, but he was several inches shorter than me, so he could never quite catch up to my pace when we played.

I hopped into the truck and started it up. My cell phone was still in the cup holder and I noticed it was blinking. I waited for the screen to brighten and clicked into my text messages. I had two waiting from Rainey.

Just got back. Remind me to never let my mother pick me up at the airport.

I laughed as I typed out a reply.

I would have been happy to pick you up ;)

I knew that would rile her up. My phone beeped almost immediately.

Not funny. You home?

I sighed. A booty call already and she'd only been back in town for less than an hour. It worked for me.

I will be in about ten minutes. Meet me?

Damn straight.

I set my phone back in the cup holder and made my way through town to my apartment. She was sitting in her mother's mini-van in the driveway when I pulled in. I smiled and threw the truck in park.

Chapter Three

Rainey

He was hot and sweaty and I loved taking advantage of him as soon as we got into his apartment.

I was on his bed, alone, after our romp while he took a shower. I was still a little out of breath after our activities. Baker was wild in bed and wasn't afraid to take sex to the next level. It was one of the things I enjoyed about him. I didn't want the emotional cuddling and pillow-talk after sex. If anything, I just wanted more sex.

So when we were finished, I wasn't the least bit offended when he headed straight for the bathroom and never said a word to me. I just yanked a sheet across my body and laid there, perfectly content. Then I realized we were going to the bar and he'd mentioned Mallory and Luke would be there, which meant Gabby and Wolfe would probably be there, too, but not together. Never together.

I needed to shower. I got up off his bed and walked across his room and into the bathroom. I pulled the shower curtain back and just stared at him.

Baker was blonde with insanely deep gray eyes. He kept his hair cropped short, but he kept a goatee around his lips, which drove me crazy. He was always giving me whisker burn, but he refused to shave it off whenever I complained. His stubbornness was sexy, even when it pissed me off. It was part of the reason I allowed myself to get entangled with him this summer. He was real and not lovey-dovey or needy. He liked to do his own thing and didn't want a commitment or to be tied down.

And since my plan was to only stay for the summer, I definitely didn't want a messy relationship to deal with. I had enough on my plate. Baker was a perfect fling for me. Our history made it almost easier, too, since we'd seen each other naked before. Of course, seeing him naked for the first time since I'd been back in Casper had been a shock.

He wasn't taller than he'd been the last time I saw him, but he had definitely filled out. His skinny arms and thighs had matured into thickly muscled limbs of steel. His abs were well-defined and hot as hell. His normally pale skin was tan and he looked rugged. I liked it.

But as I looked at him in the shower, I admired the more subtle changes in him. His face was older, more refined. He was going to be twenty-four in August and he didn't look like the kid he'd been a few years ago when we went to prom. His eyes turned a dark charcoal color as he admire my nakedness in front of him.

He didn't invite me into the shower. Instead, he lifted me into the hot spray of water and brought his lips to mine. He leaned me against the back shower wall and devoured me, his lips hot and searching. He sucked my bottom lip in between his teeth and I hissed, enjoying the slight pain as my fingers curled behind his neck.

My fingernails dug into his skin when his skilled kisses went lower, to my breasts, pulling a taut nipple into his mouth. I threw my head back in surrender and his mouth claimed my neck while his fingers tweaked my nipple. He sucked on the tender skin of my throat and I moaned, certain no one had ever made me feel like this before.

It was several minutes later that he finally stepped out of the shower so I could wash my hair. We didn't do more than make-out, since we were both still sated, but what a make-out session it had been. I used his body wash and inhaled the masculine scent, closing my eyes in appreciation. I cleaned myself thoroughly, lingering on the parts he'd lavished with kisses and touches. My skin was red and somewhat raw from his goatee. I didn't mind, though.

I spent a little extra time in the shower, relishing the hot water until a pounding on the door made me hurry.

"Rain, pick it up! I have to be at the bar in twenty minutes!" Baker shouted over the roar of the nozzle.

"Yeah, yeah," I mumbled, certain he wouldn't hear me.

I rinsed all the soap from my skin and turned off the water, then grabbed a clean towel off the shelf and flipped my head upside-down to wrap the fabric around my hair and then twist it. I straightened up, tossing the towel up over my head so it held securely, and then tucked a second towel around my body. I walked into Baker's bedroom and found him standing just a few feet from the door with his hands on his hips.

"What was that you said?"

"Uhh…" I tried to remember what smart-ass comment I'd made.

"I heard you," he said. He stalked closer to me, his towering height making me small. I backed up a step, but he grabbed my arms and pulled me forward. His lips lingered against mine. "Sometimes, you just need to do what you're told."

"Where's the fun in that?" I smirked.

He narrowed his eyes at the exposed skin of my shoulder. "Did I do that to you?" He released my arms and traced the fleshy curve of my shoulder where a bruise was already forming.

I panicked. "No, it's not from you," I lied. "I bumped into an open cabinet at my mom's today." Baker didn't know about the leukemia and I wasn't about to tell him. Too many people knew already.

But the bruise worried me. I was in remission; the bruising had stopped. Baker's rough lovemaking shouldn't turn me black and blue. I bit my lip and noticed Baker watching me carefully.

"I'm a klutz, what can I say?" I laughed it off.

He nodded but didn't look convinced. "Get dressed. I'll drive you to the bar." He turned away from me and left his bedroom.

I raced to the bathroom and used a hand towel to clear the fog that settled on the mirror. I examined the discolored patch of skin, remembering how Baker's thumb pressed into my shoulder when he held me still for his kiss. It hadn't hurt, but the proof was there in black and blue. I needed to get to the doctor's office first thing next week or Baker would be even more suspicious than he already was.

I dried off quickly and threw my clothes on. I'd worn one of my favorite tank tops, but with the bruise getting darker by the minute, I didn't want to deal with questions. Especially since it was in the precise shape of a thumb. I didn't want people thinking I was abused. So I grabbed a hoodie out of Baker's closet and carried it into the living room where he sat, waiting for me.

"What's going on?" he asked.

"What do you mean?" I played dumb.

"I know that bruise is from me, Rain. What I don't know is how the hell it showed up so fast and dark when I know I didn't hurt you."

"I just have sensitive skin," I said, not bothering to argue about how I'd gotten the bruise. He wasn't an idiot.

"No one bruises that fast," he said.

"I do. Look, it's no big deal. Don't we need to leave? I don't want you to be late." I grabbed my purse off his dining table and slung it over my shoulder. I lifted my arm and held up his hoodie. "I borrowed one of your sweatshirts."

"Of course. Gotta cover up that bruise," he mumbled sarcastically. I chose to ignore him.

He followed me out of his apartment and then opened the door for me to get into his truck. I was surprised by his gentlemanly behavior but didn't say anything. Once I was seated in the passenger seat, he came to stand next to me.

"I don't know what's going on with you, Rainey, but I don't like it. And one of these days, you're going to tell me what it is that has you bruising like a peach and getting sick at odd hours of the night." He closed the door and then hopped in the driver's seat.

I was speechless.

Baker never said a word about what was wrong with me. He didn't know exactly what it was, of course, but I thought I'd been hiding my sickness pretty well. Apparently not.

We got to the bar at six and Baker kissed me chastely and then sent me to sit with Mallory and Luke while he checked on the bar. They were cuddled up together in a corner booth. It was obvious how in love with each other they were. My heart clenched a little in jealousy. No matter how much Baker and I ever cared about each other, we weren't going to be able to have that kind of relationship.

"Hey, guys," I said as I approached the table. Just as I was about to sit down in the booth, a flurry of wild dark hair slipped past me and slid across the vinyl. "Gabby, nice to see you," I laughed as I scooted in next to her.

"What's your hurry?" Luke asked her.

"Wolfe was in the parking lot. Did you invite him?" She looked suspiciously at Luke.

"Actually, I invited him," Mallory admitted with a raised hand and a guilty look. "He's part of our little group, Gab, whether you like it or not. Besides, I thought you didn't care about what he does?" Mallory eyed Gabby.

Gabby sighed. "I don't care. I just wish he would find his own friends," she muttered. We all laughed and she gave us a little smile. When Wolfe walked up to the table, her smile faded. "We're full up," she explained, gesturing to the full booth.

"That's why I brought these," Baker said as he set two bar stools at the end of the table. "It's a little busy, guys, so I'm not sure how long I'll be able to hang out. Can I get everyone a drink?"

Mallory and Luke ordered beer while Gabby gave him some fruity, girly drink order. When Baker's eyes fell to mine, I asked for a cola. His eyes bore into mine for a full ten seconds before he turned his attention to Wolfe, who ordered a beer. Baker left the table and Wolfe sat down.

"So, what's new, Wolfe?" Luke asked. Mallory looked at Gabby and then at me.

"What are you wearing?" she asked me in shock. I was usually the best-dressed woman at the table, so wearing a hoodie was not normal.

"We had a quickie before we came over," I whispered honestly. Both sets of blue eyes widened at my bluntness and burst into giggles. Luke and Wolfe looked at us expectantly.

"Mind your p's and q's," I suggested with an evil eye and moved closer to Gabby. "We need a girls' night soon," I begged.

"Agreed." Mallory eyed Luke. "He's been keeping me on lockdown since we came back from Boston," she whispered.

Their relationship confused me immensely. Luke was mellow and laid back and Mallory was pushy but a loner. She'd wanted to deal with the death of her father alone, but Luke had finally grown a pair and backed her into a corner. She came around, though. Eventually. Plus, now that the mourning stage was finished, she was actually pretty fun to be around. She kept all the emotional crap under control until she was alone with Luke, which I appreciated. I wanted to be there for her, of course, but it wasn't like I didn't have my own shit to deal with.

She stopped complaining about her loss to me once I told her.

After the doctor's appointment in downtown Boston, I met Mallory for lunch. We shopped at Faneuil Hall for an hour and then went to the Hard Rock for a meal. I wasn't hungry, not after my treatment, but I ordered food and mentally prepared myself to tell her.

"So, I had good reason not to tell you about what was wrong with me," I started. She looked at me expectantly but didn't say anything. She knew I needed to get this all out.

"I have leukemia."

I didn't mean to blurt it out, but Mallory still didn't say anything.

"I was worried telling you so close to your dad's death would put you over the edge," I confessed. "I didn't want to add to your stress. I love you like a sister, Mallory, but I don't want to be anyone's burden. We're best friends, but I wanted to make sure you were recovering from Joe's death before I told you."

"Rainey..." She stood and walked around the table, pulling me out of my chair and hugging me. "You are one of my closest friends and I will always be there for you. I'm glad you told me," she said.

And once we sat back down, it all came spilling out... My own father's death, finding out about my leukemia, my aunt's pleas to stay away from my mother for a while. It all bubbled out and I couldn't seem to stop.

In the end, Mallory hugged me again, apologized for being too caught up in her own life to notice what was going on with me, and then promised we wouldn't keep anything from each other again.

And since then, we were closer than ever. Now that Mallory knew, we could talk about it pretty openly (except around the guys) and Gabby felt like less of a sneak, too, since she'd known for years. Mallory didn't hold it against, her, either, which I appreciated. I swore Gabby to secrecy years ago.

When Baker returned to our table with drinks on a tray, we all thanked him. He set a beer down next to me and slid his barstool close to edge of the booth on my side, then put an arm around my waist and dragged me across to seat, closer to him. I smiled up at him. He stared at me for a moment, taking in the dark circles under my eyes and his gray eyes turned cloudy as he thought about the implications.

The bar filled up fast and Baker only stayed at the table for another few minutes before he had to help out. We all ordered dinner and he brought us our meals.

"Things are good between you two, huh?" Gabby asked me once he brought us our meals and kissed me.

"Yes, they are. It's nice not to have to worry about the relationship stuff. We're just having fun and enjoying ourselves," I admitted, picking at what was left of my dinner.

"It won't work," Wolfe said from the end of the table. We all looked at him, though Gabby just rolled her eyes. "I'm not trying to ruin it for you, Rainey, but you two are eventually going to fall in love, and then you'll both run away from it, because it's not what you want. Do yourself a favor and get out now." He lifted his beer to his mouth and I watched him make eye contact with Gabby for a second before he swallowed the rest of it. He set his beer down and stood up. "Sorry to be a downer. I'll just head home," he said.

"Let us call you a cab," Luke suggested. He got out of the booth and the two of them walked over to the end of the bar and talked to Baker for a few minutes.

"What the hell was that about?" I asked Mallory and Gabby.

"Who knows?" Gabby grit her teeth. "Our marriage didn't work out, so now he wants to ruin everyone else's relationship, I guess."

"He's heartbroken, Gab. He wants you back and he can't stand seeing you happy without him," Mallory sighed.

"And who says I'm happy?" Gabby spun her fruity drink on the table. "I miss him, too. But we're too different, too set in our ways to make it work." She sniffed to hold back tears.

"Gabby, if you want a relationship to work, you have to be willing to put in the effort it takes to keep it going," Mallory said softly.

Gabby nodded but didn't reply. She kept her head down when Luke came back to the table with Baker trailing behind him.

"I think we're going to take off," Luke said. He looked at Gabby. "Want us to give you a ride home?"

Gabby looked up and gave him a quick nod. Her eyes were red and her skin blotchy, but none of us said a word. I would have to text Mallory tomorrow and see if we could put together a girl's night to figure out what was going on with Gabby.

"You want a ride too, Rainey?" Mallory asked me.

I glanced at Baker. "I think I'll just hang out here until Baker gets out of work. You don't mind giving me a ride, do you, Baker?" I asked him.

"Of course not. I've got a few things to do and then I'll take you. You want to move to the bar so we can get some more people at this table?" Baker asked. I got up with Mallory and Luke and pulled Gabby into a hug.

"We really need a girls' night," I told her. She smiled and then left with Mallory and Luke. I grabbed a stool at the end of the bar and silently watched Baker wait on customers and then head into the back to do some paperwork.

It was another hour before he was able to leave the bar. I was exhausted.

Chapter Four

Baker

I watched Rainey's head sway forward as she slept where she sat. It was hilarious.

I stood at the far end of the bar, smiling like an idiot as I watched her nod off. I knew it was late, but I couldn't change my work schedule. Besides, she knew I would make it worth her while when we got back to my place.

When her head tipped up and back, though, my heart stopped. She fell backward off the barstool and fell flat on her back. I was at her side in an instant.

"Are you okay?" I asked.

Her eyes fluttered open and she looked confused. "Baker? What happened?"

"You fell asleep at the bar," I told her. I put my hand gently under her neck and she winced. "Where does it hurt?"

"Ugh. Everywhere," she said with a groan. "I think I broke my ass."

I laughed, as did the small crowd that gathered around her.

"I'm going to take you home, okay?"

"Sounds good," she said, but made no move to get up.

I eased my arm under her shoulders and moved my other hand underneath her knees. I lifted her as carefully as I could and told Jimmy I was leaving now. He tipped his head in acknowledgement and went back to making drinks.

The crowd dispersed as soon as Rainey was off the floor. I carried her out to my truck and set her in the passenger seat, glancing at her as she rested her head back against the head rest. She looked tired. Rundown.

"I should take you to the emergency room," I suggested. Her eyes flew open in protest.

"No!"

"Alright, but you're going to stay at my place tonight, in case you have a concussion," I insisted. She didn't argue.

When we got to my apartment, I carried her in, despite her protests. Eventually she let me have my way. I set her on the couch and swung her legs up onto the cushions. When I reached for a blanket, she stopped me.

"I'm not a child," she grumbled.

"Well, you must be sick. It's only ten o'clock and you fell asleep at the bar." I wasn't letting her off the hook this time.

"I was also on a plane for most of this morning and I was up around four to catch that plane. Not to mention I hate flying." She rolled her eyes at me.

I sighed audibly and didn't hide my frustration. She was using whatever excuse she could cling to keep the truth a secret. I didn't like it, but I guessed she was safe for the time being, so I didn't push.

"Are you going to make me sleep out here or am I allowed to come to bed?" she asked. Her eyes were pure green fire; I'd upset her.

"Of course you can come to bed," I said as I moved to lift her off the couch.

"Hold it." She waved a hand at me. "I'm perfectly capable of going to the bedroom myself." She managed to get to her feet just fine, but I kept close to her as she walked to my room in case she fell. She sat on the edge of my bed and pulled off her shoes, wiggling out of her jeans and tossing my sweatshirt and her tank top on the floor. Her bra slipped off and she chucked it across the room.

She finally laid her head down on the pillow and I went into the bathroom. By the time I came back out, she was fast asleep with just a hint of a smile on her face, her hand curled underneath her chin and her body on display. She hadn't pulled the covers over herself and the sight of her took my breath away.

My eyes were drawn to her stomach, which was so flat it indented beneath her ribcage and gave her a sickly look. I frowned at her as I watched her ribcage move. There was something going on with her. And if it killed me, I would find out what it was.

***

The following morning, I woke first. I had to get to the bar and do paperwork. I stumbled into the bathroom and jumped in the shower to wash away my sleepiness. I figured Rainey would be up by the time I got out, but she was still fast asleep. I walked out into my bedroom naked, the light from the bathroom illuminating the room I'd drawn the curtains in. I walked by the bed and glanced at Rainey, who was sprawled out, face down and uncovered.

I did a double-take.

Her back was covered in big, ugly bruises that turned her skin nearly purple. I walked over to her and gently trailed my hand down her back. *What the hell? Are these from her fall last night? What is going on?*

I didn't wake her; instead, I went to my closet and pulled out clean clothes to wear.

Why was she hiding something from me? I wasn't judgmental or overprotective, so it didn't make sense why she wouldn't tell me. But then again, her thought processes were a far cry from mine. Where I was mellow and laid back, she was just a bit uptight and reserved.

She hated the small town life where everyone knows everyone else's business. Although I wasn't a fan of the whole town knowing what I was up to, I accepted it as a part of my life in Casper.

Rainey rolled over and stretched just I pulled my jeans up. I left the button undone and smiled at her. Bruises or not, she was gorgeous. Her blonde hair was wild and unruly across the pillow and she shyly pulled the sheet over herself while smiling seductively at me.

"You should come back to bed," she mumbled, still half-asleep.

I almost followed her beckoning but remembered the bruises. I didn't want to hurt her any more. I shook my head at her.

"I've got to get to work," I said as I pulled on my favorite blue T-shirt. It was thin and faded because I wore it so much.

Rainey sat up, letting the sheet fall to her waist. She leaned back on her hands, her pert breasts thrust out and taunting me. She was something else.

I walked over to the edge of the bed and leaned down to kiss her gently. She was having none of it. She curled her hand around my neck and pulled me down onto the bed. I was careful to hold my weight above her so I didn't cause any more bruises, but I couldn't resist when her tongue probed my mouth. I tipped her head back and kissed her throat. Her moans distracted me and I was just about to yank my jeans down when my mouth skimmed over the discolored skin on her shoulder.

I put that mark on her. I wasn't about to do it again. I pulled away.

"I really need to get to work. You've got your mom's minivan, right?" I asked as I stood up and stepped away from the bed. I needed to get away from her before I hurt her again.

She fell back onto the pillow. "Yeah, I'll take the minivan. I think we're going to do a girls' night tonight, so don't wait up," she explained as she hiked the sheet up to her neck. She gave me the evil eye and I knew she was pissed. It wasn't very often I refused to have sex.

"I won't," I promised and then went to fill a to-go mug with coffee. Having a self-brew coffee pot really made things easier. I skipped cream and sugar and just carried the black coffee to my truck.

I refused to feel guilty about not wanting to hurt Rainey. She was sick, and I wasn't about to add to that. I knew she'd been hiding something from me. Her whole demeanor since she'd been back was different. She was almost aloof. She wanted sex without any emotions or feelings.

Which was fine. I wasn't exactly interested in a real relationship; I was too busy for one. But I cared about Rainey, as a friend, at least. And if she was sick, I wanted her to get well, not push her limits and walk around covered in bruises. And if that meant I pissed her off, I didn't care. Her well-being came first.

I drove to the jobsite Luke was working at and hopped out of the truck, to-go mug in hand. He was on the roof of an old church in town. He spotted me and waved, making his way toward the ladder at the far end of the church. He climbed down and came over.

"Hey, man, you need work today?" he asked. On occasion, I worked for his employer, JP. I wasn't in the mood to work today, though.

"No, just needed to vent about Rainey," I muttered.

Luke looked at his watch. "It's almost ten. I can break for fifteen," he said and yelled to one of the other guys that he was taking a break. He turned back to me and motioned me to follow him to the ten-by-ten canopy that housed a picnic table.

He grabbed a couple of sodas out of the cooler and tossed one to me as we sat at the table.

"So what's up?" he asked, popping the top of his can.

"Do you know what's wrong with Rainey?" I asked. No point trying to sugar-coat it.

"I wish I did, dude. I'm almost positive Mallory knows, but she refuses to mention anything, telling me that Rainey's privacy is what's most important. But her saying that just makes me believe whatever she's hiding is kind of a big deal," he said.

His words confirmed my fears. "That's what I was afraid of. Do you think Mallory would tell me?"

Luke's head went back as he howled with laughter. "Yeah, right," he said after he finished. "Mallory is dedicated to Rainey and there's no way she'll reveal anything Rainey asked her to keep a secret. You can try, though."

I blew out a breath. "I bet you're right. But I can't help but worry about Rainey. She's acting odd and bruising easily," I said, more to myself than him.

"Bruising? How easily?" Luke turned serious and I had an inkling he might know what was going on.

"Pretty easily. She fell off her stool at the bar last night after you guys left and this morning, her whole back side was black and blue," I explained.

Luke sucked in a breath, but said nothing.

"What is it?" I asked, panicked.

"I – I can't say for sure, man, but let me talk to Rainey, okay? Maybe I can convince her to tell you whatever it is that's ailing her. You deserve to know," he commented. He closed his eyes for a minute and when he opened them, he looked almost angry, but he didn't say anything.

"Thanks, dude. I'll let you get back to work. I've got to head over to the bar, anyway. Let me know what she says when you talk to her," I said. I stood up, left my unopened can of cola at the table, and made my way back to my truck.

I worried Luke might know more than he was letting on, but if he did, I knew him well enough to know he would want to confirm his suspicions before he said anything to me. As much as I might hate that about him, I also appreciated the part where he didn't get me worked up over a possibility.

An hour later, I sat in my office at the bar, rubbing my temples. Even though business was picking up, I was still low on funds and couldn't pull a paycheck for two more weeks. And that was only if the summer crowd flooded the bar for the next ten days. I sighed, trying to figure out how I was going to make rent. I would have to work for JP on Monday and Tuesday in order to pay my household bills. I sent out a text to Luke and asked if he could use someone at the beginning of the week.

His reply came quickly, assuring me that JP could use another guy anytime I wanted. I breathed a sigh of relief and called Jimmy into my office.

"Hey, boss, what's up?" he asked from the doorway.

"Can you cover the full dayshift on Monday and Tuesday? I'm going to work for JP," I explained.

"Sure thing. I was planning on being here for most of the day, anyway. Will you work the nightshift, or do you want me to work doubles?"

"No, you can go home around five-thirty. I just need the dayshifts covered," I said. As much as I didn't want to put in two sixteen-hour days back-to-back, I couldn't afford to pay Jimmy to work doubles those days, either. So I would have to suck it up and just work. I was already tired just thinking about it.

"I wanted to ask you about time off," Jimmy said after standing there, staring at me for a full minute. I looked up at him and raised my brow in question. "My brother's wedding is the Saturday before the Fourth of July. I'd like to take that weekend off. I'm in the wedding, so I need that Friday night and Saturday, at least." He looked afraid of my answer.

"That's not a problem. I'll plan on bartending those nights so we don't get backed up. Has your brother picked a place to do his rehearsal dinner?"

"No, not yet," he replied.

"Well, tell him to give me a call and I'll give him a good deal if he comes here. And I promise you won't be required to work," I laughed.

Jimmy smiled and then took off to clean up the bar and set up the stools so they weren't still on the tabletops. In an effort to clean more efficiently, I recently dictated that the floors had to be washed thoroughly every night and then mopped with fresh-scented wood cleaner every morning. It gave the wood floors a stunning glow and the cleaner was enhanced to help protect the wood against spills and damage, which was most important.

I was just about to give up on the spreadsheet I was working on when my cell rang.

"Hello?"

"Hey, man. It's Wolfe. What's the plan for tonight? The girls are having a girls' night, apparently."

"How do you know? I only found out this morning," I wondered.

"I ran into Mallory and Rainey at the grocery store. Rainey suggested I give you a call and we hang out," he explained.

"Sounds good. Why don't you call Luke and you guys meet me at my apartment around seven?"

"Can do. See you tonight." He clicked off.

I tossed my cell on the desk and mentally dreaded the night ahead.

Chapter Five

Rainey

I spent that morning unsure of what was going on with Baker. He seemed interested in a morning quickie, but then he turned away without a second glance my way. I was pissed, but I figured he had a lot on his mind with the bar.

I'd been shocked when I walked into the bathroom and caught a glimpse of my back in the mirror. I was covered in bruises. As much as I didn't want to, I called my oncologist and explained that I was bruising easily again, a sure sign that the leukemia was back with a vengeance. He told me to come into his office that afternoon.

I showered and then grabbed a cup of coffee from Baker's kitchen. I had to pop it in the microwave for a minute before it was drinkable, but I sucked it down, still only lukewarm, and sat on the couch to lose myself in some television before my appointment.

That afternoon, I made my way to the mini-van.

My mother hadn't even noticed that I took her mini-van, but I couldn't decide if that was a good thing or a bad thing. She was probably passed out from the pills and if she had any booze, she'd be down for a while.

I started the van and drove straight to Doctor Hansen's small practice. His receptionist greeted me and then took me right into one of the examination rooms. She held up a gown and instructed me to undress and put it on.

Doctor Hansen was a short, balding man with a knack for making me laugh. Despite his humor, though, I always felt safe and informed whenever I saw him. The doctors in Boston had made me feel insignificant, so it was nice to have a doctor who actually wanted me to know as much as I possibly could about leukemia.

"Good morning, Lorraine," he greeted me by my given name, claiming he would never call me Rainey when I asked him to. It was one of the quirks I adored about him. "Let's see those bruises," he said. I pulled the back edges of the gown forward, keeping the front of my body covered and allowing him access to the discolored skin on my back. "These are pretty bad, my dear. What happened and when did they form?"

"I fell last night and they were like this when I woke up this morning," I explained.

"Alright. Let's do some blood work. These will heal, but the quickness with which they appeared worries me. I want to see what your white blood cell count is," he said. He sat at the computer in the office and moved his hands across the keys. After a few moments, he turned back to me. "So, what else is new, Lorraine? Are you seeing anyone?"

How he knew, I would never know. "Yes, sir. I've been dating Chris Baker for a couple of weeks now," I told him.

"Chris Baker. He's the fellow who bought The Landing, isn't he?" At my nod, he continued. "He's quite the hard worker. What does he have to say about the bruises?"

"He doesn't know," I said. "He actually doesn't know about the leukemia at all."

Silence.

"It's just that I don't want him to get upset over nothing. I mean, the blood work I had done in Boston last month showed an increase in white blood cells, which is good, right? I'm getting better," I said, desperate to defend my decision not to tell Baker.

"You *were* getting better, Lorraine. Things looked good a month ago, but with these bruises, I can only imagine what the blood work is going to show. We may have to discuss chemotherapy," he explained.

I groaned. The last thing I wanted was for the cancer to be back. Not to mention losing my hair would seriously damage my self-image. I mean, I knew how necessary it was, and how *not* doing it could be seriously dangerous, but I'd spent the bulk of my life being overweight. My hair was the one thing that hadn't changed – it was a long and soft, a gorgeous shade of blonde that a bottle couldn't replicate. It wasn't fair.

"I don't see any other choice," Doctor Hansen emphasized. "Now, let's get the blood work done and we can get you out of here for today."

I knew he was right. Whether I was okay with it or not, chemo was the final step in my road to recovery. Although, if the cancer was back, there wasn't much that could be done after chemo, which meant all my dreams in life weren't going to be realized.

I tried not to think about it as I had my blood drawn. I thought about my perfect summer with Baker and how it might be my last. Having an inkling that I could die was like a revelation about what mattered in life. And it wasn't my blonde hair or the fact that my mother was a druggie. All that mattered to me, at that exact moment, was Baker.

I left the doctor's office and drove straight to Mallory's house. I needed to talk to her about what the bruises meant for me. I called Gabby on the way and asked her to meet me there. It was convenient that we'd planned a girls' night, since I really needed the only two people in Casper (other than my doctor) to know about the possibility of my cancer coming back. Doctor Hansen promised I would have results in twenty-four hours, and it would be a rough day for me.

I pulled into the driveway of Mallory's home and thought of her father. Joe Wells was one of the most amazing men I'd ever known. In the short time I'd spent with him last month, I'd grown very close to him, probably because of our common cancer-filled bodies. He'd been supportive of me when I told him about the leukemia.

Mallory was grief-stricken and I felt helpless. Her father was going to die soon and there wasn't a damn thing any of us could do about it. When she went to Luke's apartment, determined that a sexual romp would release some of her pent-up anger, I went into Joe's room.

"Hey, girl. How's it going?" Joe's voice was weak and he was far too skinny. I stared at him for a moment without answering. This could be my future.

"It's going, Mr. Wells," I tried to joke, but ended up sounding more despondent than playful.

"Sit down, Rainey. Tell me what's wrong," he demanded.

I swallowed hard and took a seat in the chair next to his bed. "I don't know where to start," I admitted.

"Start at the beginning," he replied. He placed his hand over mine and I was immediately comforted.

"Well, I guess that would be when my dad died. And I don't need any reassurances or comfort about his death," I said quickly, when it looked like he was going to say something about my dad. "I'm okay with his death. But after I went back to LA, I found out I had leukemia."

"Well, I didn't see that coming," Joe said.

"So my aunt encouraged me to stay there, where they have some great doctors, and I wouldn't be burdened with trying to keep all my friends happy and not worried about me. It was easier to deal with everyone long-distance. Gabby is the only one I told about the cancer. And now, I'm afraid to tell Mallory – she's not exactly handling the news of your cancer very well."

"I agree that you should keep Mallory in the dark. She's still dealing with my sickness, and soon, she'll have to deal with my death. But there will come a time when she's going to need to hear it and you're going to have to tell her. And I think you'll know when the time comes. But back to you. Are you afraid of what the leukemia will do to you?" Joe asked.

"Yes and no. I mean, so far, it's under control and the doctors haven't told me to say my goodbyes or anything, but it's still there, lurking in the shadows. I'm afraid to say goodbye."

"It's hard, Rainey, but not impossible. Once you accept your fate. You can help others deal with your death, even before it happens. Cancer patients have the coveted advantage of knowing they're going to die, whereas most people don't. You have a chance to inspire the people around you, not to mourn your death, but rather celebrate your life. And I think that is something worthwhile," he said.

His words really hit home. I wanted to talk to him some more, but he fell asleep. It was the last conversation I had with him.

Joe was the one person who understood my issues completely. Eventually, I told Mallory about the leukemia, and she and Gabby were supportive, but they didn't understand the disease. They didn't know how many times I had to force myself to get up in the morning when I would rather lay in bed and sleep all day. They didn't understand that drinking alcohol usually made me violently ill or that I often got extremely tired for no reason at all.

This life was a burden, one I wouldn't wish on my worst enemy. I didn't have to wish it on someone else, though; it was just for me: my own personal hell. I tried to ignore the facts and focus on living whatever life I had left to the fullest. I didn't want to count my chickens before they hatched.

I pulled into Mallory's driveway and made my way inside. The house still smelled a little like Joe and I smiled at the immediate memories his scent brought to my mind.

"Hello?" I called into the seemingly empty house. When I got no answer, I checked outside for Mallory's car. It wasn't there. Instead of leaving, I made myself comfortable. I sat on the couch and pulled my smartphone out of my purse, clicking through the apps until I had a book on the screen. I had a distinct love of reading and tried to get in as much time as I could with a good book.

It was a while later, when the sun was just starting its descent into western horizon that the front door swung open. I jumped.

"Hey, Rainey," Luke said from the doorway.

I turned toward him. "Hi, Luke. I'm just waiting for Mallory," I explained.

"I figured. She had to work at the bank late, but I just got off the phone with her and she should be home in a few minutes. Actually, do you have a minute to talk?" He walked through the living room to the extra-large recliner in the corner and sat down.

"Sure," I said, putting my phone back in my purse and giving him my attention.

He locked his hands together with elbows resting on his knees, a gesture that reminded me so much of Joe.

"What's going on, Rainey?"

"What do you mean?"

"Don't play dumb. I watched cancer slowly kill Joe for years. Do you really think I wouldn't recognize the signs? I'm not letting it go anymore. You either tell me right now or I take my suspicions to Baker," he threatened.

"No! Please don't," I begged. Tears welled up in my eyes and I tried to reign them in. "It's not what you think."

"Oh? Then tell me what it is," he suggested.

"Uhh," I tried to think of something, but my mind came up blank.

"Don't lie to me, Rainey. I'm your friend and I don't really understand why you're hiding this from everyone," he said. His blue eyes turned sad, almost fearful.

"I'm not hiding it from *everyone*," I emphasized. "I just don't want Baker to know. It's not wrong of me to want one perfect summer before…"

"Before…you die?" Anger flashed in his eyes and he stood. "Tell me what it is."

"I have leukemia," I whispered, not looking at him.

Luke sat back down. "Rainey, I'm sorry that you are going through this, but all of us care about you, and we should have known. You need to tell Baker."

"No! I can't," I said. "He won't understand, Luke. You remember how it was with Joe – he couldn't tell Mallory for years because of the guilt he felt. That's how I feel now. I don't want Baker to know."

"You're being selfish," he said, rising off the recliner again. "I won't let you do this to him, Rainey. He's already half in love with you and this will cut him deep when he finds out. And he *will* find out. He's not an idiot – he already came to me wondering what was up because of the bruises. Not to mention that this is a small town, which means eventually someone will let it slip to the wrong person and everyone will know. And how will that make Baker feel to find out about you from the gossips in town instead of you? You've got a choice to make. I'll give you a week to tell him the truth or I will," he said. He stomped out of the room, effectively cutting off any other arguments I could summon.

He was right; I needed to tell Baker. I hoped he would understand.

Chapter Six

Baker

When I finally made it back to my apartment, I was exhausted and definitely not in the mood to deal with a guys' night. But Luke and Wolfe were already waiting for me, so I couldn't exactly kick them out, as much as I wanted to. They were standing in front of Luke's truck in the driveway, deep in discussion when I pulled in. I opened the truck door and nodded to them.

"Hey, what's up?" I asked as I climbed out. I slammed the door closed, more out of habit than frustration, but they both raised a brow at me. "It closes hard." They both looked appeased.

"What's on the agenda?" Wolfe asked as they followed me up the stairs into my apartment.

My apartment was above a small pool hall, and although I sucked at the game, I didn't want to be stuck at my place. I needed a beer and a little bit of relaxation.

"How about we play a few rounds of pool?" I suggested.

Both of them looked amused. "Trying to take your mind off Rainey?" Luke asked. I rolled my eyes but didn't comment. He was right, of course, but I wasn't about to give him the satisfaction of knowing.

"Let's go," I said instead. I left the apartment without so much as a backward glance and walked into the pool hall.

I order three beers from the bartender and then paid for a table. I had the balls racked up and beers waiting by the time Wolfe and Luke made it downstairs. No doubt they took an extra minute up there to discuss me. I took a long swallow off my beer and grabbed a cue.

"You going to girl-talk all night or play pool?" I grinned at them, lining up the break. Of all my lacking pool skills, I could break like no one else I knew. It was my best chance at winning.

"Who said you get to break?" Luke protested as I slammed the white ball with the cue and it went sailing into the group of colored and striped balls, spreading them out across the table. Two dropped into a corner pocket and I laughed.

"I break because I never get any balls after the break," I admitted. Both of them were aware of my shitty pool skills and were probably wondering why on earth I would choose to play pool instead of poker or something.

The truth was, the loud music in the pool hall drowned out my thoughts of Rainey and the loud cracking of the balls slamming together filled my head instead of thinking about Rainey's secret. She was important to me, but I didn't want to allow myself to get too close. She'd made herself very clear at the beginning of our little arrangement, informing me that this was to be just a summer fling and nothing more. It didn't matter that I had feelings for her; she wouldn't have it.

"Hello? Earth to Baker." Luke waved a hand in front of my face and I realized I was poised to shoot but I hadn't moved in several seconds.

"Whoops," I said, lining up my next shot again and then whipping the cue into the white ball.

It careened off the table and onto the green felt top of the pool table two rows over. It bounced once and then rolled into the side pocket of that table. Lucky for me, it didn't hit anyone and there wasn't anyone playing at that table. Wolfe and Luke erupted into riotous laughter as I made my way across the place and grabbed the ball before anyone else noticed my mishap. The glaring bartender let me know that she had seen. I grinned like a fool at her and made my way back to our table.

"Shut up," I demanded of my friends. They could hardly contain themselves. I ignored them and set the ball down on the table. "One of you just take a damn shot." I walked over to the small pub table against the wall and sipped from my beer.

Luke stepped up to the pool table and lined up a shot. Wolfe finally quieted down and came to stand next to the pub table. He rested both his hands on the top of his cue and looked at me pointedly.

"How's things with Rainey?" he asked.

"What do you mean?"

"Well, Luke told me about her keeping a secret," he explained.

"Real subtle, Wolfe. Play the damn game," Luke said, walking away from the pool table after his missed shot and pushing Wolfe away from the pub table.

"I'm going." He shrugged Luke off and lined up his shot.

"So you told Wolfe before you told me?" I glared at Luke.

"I didn't tell him anything. He asked about you and Rainey and I just told him that you thought Rainey was hiding something. That's *all* I told him," he said with a glare at Wolfe.

"So what's she hiding?"

"Unfortunately, I can't tell you," he started. At my look of surprise, he continued. "I *will* tell you, if she doesn't. But I've given her a week to work up the courage to tell you. And when she does, man, you've got to try to be understanding, because it's not something that's easy to discuss with someone. Trust me, I know," he said.

I sighed. "I guess I don't have a choice then. I'm not going to give up on her, so that means waiting for her to trust me enough to tell me the truth." I sipped my beer and Wolfe approached. "Does everyone but me know?"

"Not really. Wolfe doesn't know," Luke said with a grin.

"Hey, not for lack of trying, though. Gabby's not talking to me right now, so I am currently shit out of luck for knowing gossip," he said.

"What's with the on-again, off-again thing you and Gabby have going?" Luke asked him.

"Oh, that. She runs hot and cold. She loves me one minute and hates me the next. It's frustrating and it really makes me want to walk away, but I love her, so I'm stuck. For the time being, I'm just happy for any time she wants to spend with me," Wolfe explained.

Wolfe and Gabby were going through a divorce, but the judge had demanded they go to counseling and try to work on their marriage for an entire year before they would be granted a divorce. It was something to do with them being so young when they married and the fact that the judge was anti-divorce.

Theirs was an odd situation and I definitely wouldn't want to be in it, but I did feel for Wolfe. He was in love with his wife and she couldn't make up her mind how she felt about him. It was sad, really. But it was their problem to deal with, and Wolfe wasn't a huge fan of discussing the intimate details of his marriage, so I only knew bits and pieces from what Rainey had heard from Gabby.

"I totally get that hot and cold thing," I told Wolfe. "Rainey claims she doesn't want anything more than a fling, but she sleeps over almost every night, regardless of whether I have to work the next day or not. It's like having a live-in girlfriend who doesn't want to actually *be* my girlfriend," I sighed.

Another round of laughter started and I ignored them. They called me a girl and then drank their beers, talking amongst themselves while I took another shot. When I walked back over to them, they stopped talking and Luke went to take his next shot.

"If you guys are going to talk about me, the least you could do is include me," I muttered under my breath.

Beer flew out of Wolfe's mouth as he tried to hold back a laugh while he drank from his beer. The floor was soaked and I shook my head in disgust, but didn't say anything more. I wished someone would put me out of my misery.

"Listen, Baker," Luke said as he approached the table and grabbed his beer. "We are never going to understand women. *Never ever*. If you accept that, you'll live a much happier life, I promise."

I rolled my eyes, but he made sense. Rainey was someone whose behaviors and attitudes I was never going to be able to predict. She was a hellcat and every minute with her was time spent on my toes. She had a great sense of humor and she got weepy late at night when she thought I was asleep, but I didn't get why. Luke was right; I wasn't going to understand her.

"So, I should just enjoy the ride?" I asked.

"Oh, she likes to ride? Good to know," Wolfe joked.

"Some women are domineering," Luke laughed.

I couldn't help but laugh along. "Shut up. My sex life is none of your business," I informed them. "But if it was, you'd know that I've never been with anyone like Rainey," I boasted.

"Oh, now you *have* to tell us," Wolfe begged. "You can't leave us with a juicy piece of info like that and then just cut us off."

"She's just a little wild, you know? She takes what she wants and she's not afraid to tell me exactly what it is she wants me to do," I said.

"Nice," Luke chuckled.

"Damn. Gabby's more reserved in the bedroom. Of course, it's been a long time since she and I were even in a bedroom together," Wolfe said wistfully.

"Can we stop with all the girl talk and get to this stupid pool game?" I asked, making my way back to the pool table.

"It's my turn." Wolfe pushed me back against the pub table and our beer bottles would have fallen if Luke hadn't been fast enough to catch them.

Wolfe laughed and took his spot at the pool table while I hung back and took my beer from Luke.

"You think you and Mallory will ever get married?" I asked, suddenly curious about it.

Luke choked on his beer. "I'm not sure. I mean, watching Wolfe and Gabby go through what they're going through makes me nervous, you know? They used to be happy, and now they can hardly stand each other most days. It's heartbreaking and I'm not sure I want to experience that," he answered.

"But what about love and all that?" I asked, watching Wolfe sink a ball in the corner pocket and then line up another shot.

"I know. It's a confusing thing. I love Mal, but we haven't talked about marriage and I'm not sure we will for a while. She's still mourning Joe's death – hell, we all are. He wasn't someone you forget easily," Luke said.

I couldn't help but agree. My mind drifted back to one conversation Joe and I had before his death.

Rainey was back in town and completely ignoring me. As much as I wanted to ask her out, I was a little afraid of rejection. She was the one person who shook the foundation of my very soul when she walked back into town. Seeing her for the first time after all those years was like someone put a vice around my heart and tightened it so that my heart just exploded inside my chest. She was beautiful in every possible way, inside and out. And I was a fool to think she would ever have anything to do with me.

Joe Wells was on his deathbed at home and I needed some guidance. He was the smartest guy I knew.

"Chris, good to see you, son," Joe greeted me. He refused to call me by my last name like everyone else I knew.

"Mr. Wells, I'm glad you're awake," I said, shaking his frail hand.

"Sit down, sit down. Let's chat," he suggested. Once I was seated, he smiled at me. "What's new, boy?"

It usually bothered me when people called me boy, but with Joe, it was appropriate. "I'm just trying to figure out what the hell to do about Rainey," I blurted.

"Ah... Mallory told me Rainey was back in town and I wondered when you would see her," he said.

"Yeah, I ran into her at The Landing last night and made a complete fool of myself," I admitted. "She probably thinks I'm a dumbass."

Joe chuckled. "Probably. But ever there were two people who belonged together, it's you and Rainey. The way you two clicked when she was in high school wasn't a fluke. The two of you are meant to be, Chris. I suggest you do whatever is necessary to make it right and don't give up on her. Never, you hear me? No matter what obstacles you face, stand by her side," he commanded.

I had nodded my agreement and then the conversation turned to something more menial. I blew out a breath and decided right there in the bar that I would heed Joe's words. I would stand by Rainey no matter what her secret was, no matter if I was hurt by her or not. Joe was right; Rainey and I were meant to be and I wasn't about to let her slip through my fingers.

Chapter Seven

Rainey

Our girls' night started out like any other night and although it was just the three of us, we had a great time. We discussed the men in our lives, although, really, Mallory was the only one truly happy with the man in her life.

"So, I have to tell you guys something," I started as they poured wine. I declined the offer and stuck to water, which was guaranteed not to make me sick.

"Oh, gossip! Do tell." Gabby scooted closer to me on the couch.

"It's not gossip, per se, but I've been bruising pretty easily lately, and my doctor had me have some blood drawn today to check things out," I confessed.

"What! Oh no," Mallory said, moving over to the floor in front of the couch and putting her arm on my knee.

Gabby grabbed my hand and squeezed. "We're here for you," she said.

I smiled at them. "I know. Believe it or not, I'm okay with however the results turn out," I assured them. It was the truth. Life or death wasn't really a big deal to me anymore. I accepted the fact that I would probably die much younger than anyone else I knew and whatever happened was meant to be. "The problem is, I think Baker knows," I explained.

"Oh. Well, why don't you tell him?" Gabby suggested.

"I think that's a great idea," Mallory said as she patted my leg. "He deserves to know."

"I know I should. The problem is, now I'm under a time restraint to tell him, because of Luke."

"What does Luke have to do with anything?" Mallory asked.

"Well, Baker must have seen the bruises on my back and he mentioned something to Luke. So Luke confronted me and demanded that I tell Baker. He said he was giving me a week to tell him or he was going to," I said.

"That doesn't sound like something Luke would say," Gabby protested.

"He's bluffing," Mallory announced.

"I don't think he is, Mal. He looked angry with me for keeping this away from Baker," I said.

"Well, I imagine he's thinking about how hard I took the news of Dad's cancer – Dad kept it from me for years and I didn't have any idea. It was rough to face it at the very last minute and I didn't have a whole lot of time to grieve," Mallory said.

Gabby nodded. "Something that neither of you saw was the effect of Joe's cancer on Luke. He watched the man he looked up to most – I mean, Joe was like a father to Luke… And Luke watched his body deteriorate and his health fail for a long time. It was hard on him. He held resentment toward you,

Mal, and even though you guys have worked everything out, the stress of dealing with Joe all by himself wore him out, both mentally and physically. So when he gets mad at you, Rainey, he's probably thinking about all the time he wished he could share his burdens with someone. He also probably knows that Joe would have been better off if Mallory had known sooner. He would have been able to spend more time with his daughter before he died."

"So even though he's angry with you, what he's saying is true. He doesn't want Baker to resent you the way he resented Mallory for a long time. Of course, Mallory never knew, and so they were able to work it out, but Baker knows something is going on... How is he going to feel when he finds out it's leukemia? That you're *dying*," Gabby stressed.

"Gabby! Not cool," Mallory chastised her.

"Nope, you don't get to judge me, Mallory. You, of all people, should know the importance of being able to say your goodbyes. Especially considering that if your dad had died any sooner, you never would have been able to forgive yourself for not being there. And no matter what those test results show, the end result is your death, Rainey. Whether it's tomorrow or five years from now, or fifteen years from now. And Baker truly cares about you. He's not going to be okay with being left in the dark this long. You two have been dating for weeks. He has a right to know, and I am one hundred percent with Luke on this. You need to tell Baker, the sooner the better."

Gabby crossed her arms over her chest, a dare for either me or Mallory to challenge her. As much as I wanted to, I couldn't argue with her logic. She was absolutely right. And that meant I needed to tell Baker about the leukemia.

I nodded to Gabby. "I'll tell him tomorrow, after I get the test results. And," I added when it looked like she was going to protest, "I'll tell him whether I get good news or bad."

Mallory kept quiet but squeezed my knee again. I suggested we watch a movie and Gabby moved to put a disc in the Blu-Ray player.

We spent the next hour and a half watching Tom Cruise as Maverick. When Luke walked in the front door, we all looked at him expectantly.

"I don't mean to interrupt," he said, throwing his hands up in defense. "I'm just going to go to bed. Goodnight, babe." He walked over and placed a kiss on Mallory's forehead and then walked back to the room they shared.

"I guess that's our cue to get out of here," Gabby said.

"You guys don't have to," Mallory protested, but I could see her looking down the hall with anticipation.

I smiled. "We'll go, Mal. And we'll talk to you tomorrow," I promised.

Gabby and I got up off the couch and made our way outside. Before I got into the mini-van, Gabby put a hand on my shoulder.

"I'm sorry I was so harsh, Rain," she apologized.

"Don't apologize, Gabby. One of the reasons we are such good friends is that we're always honest with each other. I wouldn't trade that for anything," I replied. I pulled her close and hugged her. "Love you, Gabby," I said in her ear.

"I love you, too, babe. No matter what you decide about Baker," she said as she pulled away from the hug. "Remember that he only has your best interests at heart. He cares about you."

I smiled at her words, more certain than ever that she was right. This thing with Baker might have started out as a fling, but it was quickly turning into more than that, whether I wanted it to or not. Baker was important to me, and if had a secret like mine, I would probably brow-beat him until he told me the whole story. So the fact that he was being patient and understanding only proved that he was the kind of guy I should be with. Not to mention he was incredible in bed.

I grinned like an idiot as I thought about his lovemaking skills and got into the driver's seat of my mother's mini-van. Maybe I would go over to his place tonight and surprise him with a good romp. And then promise him that I would tell him. I just needed a bit more time to work up the courage.

When I pulled into the driveway, I was surprised to see all the lights off in his apartment. But the outside light was on, a beacon of invitation to me; no matter how unsure he was about us, he always made sure I felt like I mattered. I sat there in the driveway for several minutes, thinking about how lucky I was to have a guy like Baker. He was pleasant and good-natured with an amazing sense of humor. He could always make me laugh.

I got out and walked up the steps, opening the front door like I belonged there and walking straight into his bedroom. He was laying on his bed, propped up with an extra pillow and doing something with his phone. He looked up when he saw me and his face lit up, even more than it already was from the glow of the screen. I smiled in reaction and paused at the threshold, taking the time to just stare at him. He was naked, but partially covered by the sheet pulled across his legs. His arms were thick with muscle, his chest broad and tan. His waist was trim and narrow, his hips almost non-existent beneath the cover of the sheet.

He tilted his head at me. "See something you like?" He pulled the sheet down just a bit more and I could feel my body tingle at the idea of getting my hands on him.

"Not yet, I don't," I said as I walked over to the bed. "But I will." I yanked the sheet off the end of the bed, revealing his beautiful naked body, and had to step back from the impact. I had seen him naked plenty of times, but each time was like the first, taking my breath away.

Unfortunately for me, I stepped on the edge of the sheet that was hanging from my hand. My body jerked unnaturally and my foot twisted in the thin fabric. Even as my brain told my hand to let go of the sheet, I clutched it tighter. The force of my grip on the sheet caused both my feet to come out from under me. I fell backwards, my ass slamming into the hardwood floor and then my head making a resounding crack against the wood. I closed my eyes in utter humiliation.

When I opened them, Baker was standing near me, leaned over so his head was close to mine. There was an unmistakably glitter in his eyes as he tried to hide his smile.

"Do you have a problem staying on your feet?" he asked.

"You know, most guys would like a woman who constantly found herself on her back," I retorted.

He snorted in laughter. "Touché. I prefer to be the one on my back, though," he said as he offered me a hand up.

I couldn't even grip his hand, I was laughing so hard. I managed to sit up and he sat next to me.

"I wasn't sure you'd come by tonight," he whispered once the laughter died down.

"I wasn't sure I would, either. But I wanted you to know something," I started. Baker sucked in a breath in anticipation, obviously expecting the worst. "I'm going to tell you what's up with me. I know that sounds lame, but I *will* tell you. I just need a couple more days, okay?"

"Take all the time you need, Rainey. I don't expect you to share everything with me. But the fact that you want to, even if you don't know how, makes all the difference. I would wait a thousand years to listen to something you had to tell me."

My heart clenched and I drew his face closer to mine, anxious to kiss him and end this conversation that was precariously close to turning even more serious. I set my lips on his and when he gathered me in his arms, I knew he agreed with me about the conversation. He tasted like beer and I moaned into his mouth, loving every taste of him. His hands went to my hair, gripping my head and pulling me closer.

When I put my arms around his waist, I realized belatedly that he was naked and I was completely dressed. I started to giggle.

"Something funny?" he asked, nibbling the fullness of my lower lip.

"Well, I'm still fully clothed and you're…not," I giggled again.

Baker laughed against me, his shoulders shaking my body. "Let's remedy that, then," he suggested, rising up off the floor and helping me stand.

When I was upright, he undid the button and zipper of my jeans, pushing the material off my hips and down my legs. I stepped out of them and he made his way back to me, his hands trailing softly across my body. Goosebumps formed on my skin and I shivered with excitement. He slowly unbuttoned my shirt, paying extra attention to the chest area. My nipples strained against the fabric as he rubbed them through it. He grinned at me, enjoying watching me squirm in his arms.

He finally finished and pushed my shirt off my shoulders, letting it hit the floor. I stood there before him, almost completely naked, and felt a little self-conscious. My body had never been perfect, and I still wasn't used to having a smaller figure now, even though it had been a while since I lost the weight.

As if picking up on my reservations, Baker called my attention. "Rainey, look at me. You are so exquisite, so beautiful I can barely keep my hands off you whenever I'm near you. But your beauty has little to do with your looks and the most to do with this," he said, putting his palm over my heart.

My throat closed. How had I been lucky enough to attract this man? He was absolutely perfect, my exact match in nearly every way. Baker would walk through the fires of Hell for me, if I asked him to. Tears welled up in my eyes and everything went blurry.

"Don't cry, baby," he said, wiping a tear from my cheek. "You are truly beautiful." Baker slipped his arm beneath my legs and lifted me up in his arms. My hands went around his neck and I smiled at him. He walked around the bed, careful to avoid the killer sheet, and set me on the mattress. He jumped over me onto the bed, making us both bounce.

I laughed and more tears escaped my eyes.

Chapter Eight

Baker

I wiped more tears from her cheeks and smiled at her. Rainey was, without a doubt, the most beautiful woman I'd ever encountered. She returned my smile and I leaned down to kiss her gently. Even though I was primed and ready for a romp in the sack, I wanted her to know that what was between us was more than just sex for me.

So I rolled onto my back and dragged her over to me so that her head was cradled in the crook of my neck. Her left hand trailed down my chest toward my erection, but I grabbed her hand and brought it back up to my chest.

I kissed her forehead. "Let's just enjoy each other's company," I suggested. I heard her sigh and smiled with satisfaction.

Whether she liked it or not, I would make her fall in love with me before the summer ended. And I'd make her mine forever. If that meant moving to LA with her in the fall, I was okay with that, too. The bar was stressful and I was positive I could find a job in LA without any problems. I shook my head at my thoughts. I hadn't even told her I loved her yet and I was planning our future together. But I did love her.

I loved her so much my heart ached every time I looked at her pretty green eyes, every time I heard her infectious laughter – she was perfect. If she needed time, I was okay with it, but there was no way I was letting her go again. When she moved to LA, I wished I had the courage to tell her about the way I felt about her then, but it wasn't meant to be...yet. Once she told me her news, I would tell her how much I loved her, how she was the sun in my life, shining her brightness into the dark recesses of my body and soul.

Rainey curled into me, rubbing her face across my chest.

"How do you always know the right thing to say?" she whispered with a sigh. Her eyes were closed and my grin widened as I rolled my eyes.

"I don't. But it's good that you think so," I replied. Her body rumbled next to mine as she stifled a laugh. We fell asleep, wrapped in each other's arms.

The next morning, I woke to fins her staring at me.

"Tell me something," she demanded.

"Anything."

"When I tell you, do you promise not to freak out?"

I didn't answer her right away. The seriousness of her tone suggested she was completely serious, and although I had never *freaked out* about anything in my life, I wasn't so sure I could make that promise.

"Define *freak out*."

She laughed nervously. "You know, like tell me I'm an idiot or yell at me, or even... Leave me." She looked somber and I wanted to smother her fears.

"Well I sure as hell won't *leave* you, Rainey. We have a pretty good thing going, don't you think?"

"I do. Which is why I'm worried that you'll leave once you know," she trailed off, her eyes closing again.

"If you're dreading it so much, just tell me," I demanded, angry with myself for already pushing the subject when I told her I wouldn't. I just couldn't help myself.

"I *can't*." Her voice broke and she pulled away from me, sitting up and wrapping her arms around her knees. She shivered.

"Rainey, you do realize that this isn't just some damn summer fling for me, right?" I asked, as close as I would get to admitting that I loved her. "I want us to be together for more than just a few weeks in the sunshine."

She turned to glare at me. "No, Baker. That's not how this works. We only agreed to a summer fling and I am not about to get caught up in the idea that we could be together for any amount of time, because it's just not possible!" She got up off the bed and threw on one of my T-shirts. It reached the tops of her thighs, effectively covering her body. When she turned back to me, her eyes were pools of emerald fire.

"Let's get one thing straight, Chris Baker – I am in control of this relationship. I say when it ends, not you!" she spat. I knew I must look like an idiot, staring at her, slack-jawed and silent, but I had a hard time wrapping my head around her words.

Here I was, deep in love with this woman and she was pushing me away *again*, and there was nothing I could say to derail this tragic train wreck. So I let my anger get the best of me.

"Of course it is, Rainey. You're wrong on one aspect, though – this isn't a relationship." I stalked toward her and she covered her naked body protectively. I put my face close to hers and enunciated every word. "A real relationship doesn't involve massive amounts of control by one person and forcing the other person to do whatever she wants him to do. I'm not some brainless oaf who you can just push around. You don't get to just make me fall in love with you and then stomp all over me like a heartless bitch!" I stormed into the bathroom and slammed the door so hard the mirror shook.

I turned on the sink and splashed cold water over my burning face. My pulse raced and I stared at myself in the mirror, noting my left eyelid twitching uncontrollably. My breaths were ragged, my fists clenched at my sides so tight my fingernails bit into my palms. I knew I shouldn't have gotten into her space. The worst part was, I didn't have any excuse.

Anger was hardly a new sensation to me, but this fierce possessiveness I felt toward Rainey was novel to me. I was a self-proclaimed perpetual bachelor – when did I turn into some lovesick pup? I might not like it, but I could hardly do anything to control my feelings for her. She was an amazing woman and I was an ass for treating her that way.

With a deep breath, I shut off the running water and opened up the bathroom door, ready to apologize for my behavior.

My bedroom was empty. Even though my gut told me Rainey wasn't somewhere else in the apartment, I searched the living room and kitchen anyway. She was gone.

Smooth move, Baker. Real smooth.

Chapter Nine

Rainey

I ran out of Baker's apartment and had no idea where to go. My first reaction was to go to Mallory or Gabby, but they wanted me to be with Baker and they would probably side with him. Hell, they pretty much already had. And so had Luke. They all thought I should tell Baker and they pushed and pushed until I had broken.

I wasn't in a place to make undying vows of love to Baker, even though he clearly had feelings for me. My shock at his announcement of falling in love with me had gone unnoticed as he continued his tirade. When he went into the bathroom, I booked it out of there as fast as I could, afraid of him. Not physically, of course. Baker would never lay a hand on me, but his love was fierce and demanding, two things I just couldn't handle right now.

Maybe if you told him about the leukemia, he wouldn't push so hard, a voice said in the back of my mind.

Shut up.

And now I was talking back to the voices in my head. I must be clinically insane. The leukemia was obviously messing with my brain function.

I blew out a labored breath and continued to run. I made a left on Standpipe Road and realized I was only a mile away from the farm house Wolfe was renting. I might not want to talk to someone, but the truth was, I needed a non-partial party to vent to. And since a therapist wasn't available, Wolfe would be the next best thing.

Six minutes later, I knocked on his door and rested my hands on my knees on his porch, trying to regulate my breathing.

The heavy oak door swung open. "Rainey?"

"Hey, Wolfe," I said as I looked up.

His tall stance was only barely framed by the door. He probably had to duck his head to go through the doorway and I smiled at the thought. I had never paid much attention to him before, mostly because he was Gabby's husband, which meant he was off-limits. His green eyes were darker than my own, more aged and wiser. They were in stark contrast to his jet-black hair that was long enough to remind me of Shaggy from the Scooby-Doo cartoon I'd watched as a kid.

He smiled at me. "Come on in," he said, pushing the screen door open with a loud creak.

"Thanks," I replied. I wandered into his house and noticed it was not well lived in. There were no pictures hanging on the walls, no frames adorning the bookshelves that lined the far wall. There were, however, plenty of books. Aside from the bookshelves, paperbacks lined the two end tables and even the small round kitchen table.

"Sorry about the mess," Wolfe mumbled as he cleared away some space at the table. I stifled a laugh as I watched him haphazardly carry an armload of books to the coffee table in front of the couch. "Please sit." He gestured to the wooden chairs at the table and dropped a few books onto the floor.

"Do you want some help?" I moved toward him but his glare stopped me.

"Stay right there!" he commanded. He tried to ease the remaining books onto the table but finally got fed up and just tossed them on the couch. "Fuck it," I heard him mumble. He turned to me with a smile. "Want something to drink?"

I couldn't hold it in any longer and laughed out loud. "Sure," I managed to get out in between laughs and gasps for air.

Wolfe grinned and went to the fridge, pulling out a bottle of water and a beer. He held both out for me to choose. I grabbed the water and he popped the tab on his brew and plopped down in the chair next to mine.

"So what's up, girl?" He took a long swig of his beer and then eyed me suspiciously.

"I don't know. I just needed to vent to someone, and not the usual someone," I confessed.

"Finally. Does this mean I get to know your secret?" he asked hopefully.

"How do you know I have a secret?" I was incredulous. I thought I hid it well.

"Oh, come on, Rain. You can't be serious…" He stared me down for a few moments, gauging my response. "Okay, first, you never drink, and when you do, it makes you sick. Second, you went to Boston for 'work.'" He used air quotes around the word *work*. "Plus, you don't seem all that healthy."

79

I was ready to combat him verbally until he said that. "What? I'm at the lowest weight I've ever been," I argued.

"That's what I mean. Gabby has photo albums of you guys as teenagers and you look vibrant and healthy. Now, you sort of look like Joe did. Sallow and sickly."

He spoke so matter-of-factly that I couldn't reply right away. Obviously, I wasn't hiding my illness as well as I thought.

"You're right. I have leukemia," I told him.

His brows rose. "I didn't think it was *that* bad," he whispered, pushing his beer away and grabbing my hand. "What are they doing for you?"

"Everything they can. It was controlled very well for a while, but now it seems to be back, although I haven't confirmed that with the doctors yet. I was tested the other day but haven't heard back yet," I explained.

"Have you told Baker?"

"No."

"Why not?" he questioned.

"I'm not sure," I answered. It was the most honest answer I had. I didn't really *know* why I was so adamant that Baker not know exactly what was going on with me.

"Well, you probably ought to tell him. Imagine if you died and he never knew the truth."

"Wolfe! That's a little rude," I reprimanded him. I pulled my hand away from his grasp.

"Bullshit. That's the real world. How would *you* feel if he had cancer and never told you and then he died one day without ever telling you the truth? You'd resent him," he said.

I looked away from his burning eyes, knowing he was right. I fidgeted with the paper label of my water bottle and bit my lip. He was right, of course. I didn't want to admit it to him, but his words were plain as day.

"I'm not trying to be an ass, Rainey." Wolfe reached over and squeezed my hand again. "I'm just pointing out what it would be like for you if the situation was reversed."

Tears pricked my eyes and I blinked them away. I glanced up at him and saw no pity, only understanding. He was a man who *had* lost the one woman he wanted in life, so he knew exactly how Baker would feel if he lost me. My heart flip-flopped in my chest at the thought of Baker mourning me. He would never forgive me, or himself, for that matter.

"You're right," I whispered. I put my head in my hands and let the tears fall.

I could feel Wolfe's growing awkwardness as I cried in front of him. He patted my back uncomfortably while I sobbed. If I wasn't so dejected and depressed, I might find it hilarious that Wolfe was trying to soothe me. Out of the corner of my eye, I saw him stare at the ceiling while he pet my shoulder like he would a cat.

I wanted nothing more than to be alone, but I was grateful for Wolfe's presence. His odd way at comforting me was actually working. My chest ached with the weight of a thousand pounds, but the tears eventually slowed and stopped. I rubbed my puffy red eyes and chanced a glance at him.

Wolfe smiled at me. "Better?"

"Actually, yes," I replied.

"Thank God," he groaned, pulling his hand away from me and walking over to the living room to fetch a box of tissues. He handed them to me and leaned against the counter in his kitchen while I wiped the tears away in an attempt to not look like I'd just been crying.

"How do I look?" I asked him, planting a weak smile on my face and staring at him intently.

Wolfe didn't miss a beat. "Gorgeous," he responded with a straight face. I could see the glimmer of a smirk under his serious expression, though.

I burst into laughter. "You are something else," I said, more tears squeezing out under my eyes. At least these weren't the depressed tears.

"I try," he commented. He walked over to me and pulled me up to stand. He wiped away a stray tear from my cheek and looked me in the eye. "Are you okay?"

The concern in his voice coupled with the fear in his eyes had me smiling at him. "I'm fine, Wolfe. I will eventually get through this. And I *will* tell Baker," I promised.

He nodded at me and pulled me in for a hug. We stood there for several minutes and I let go of all the stress I'd been holding tightly to over the last few weeks.

Joe's death had been particularly difficult for me, mostly because it made me realize my own mortality. Add the stress of a new relationship, even with someone as easy-going as Baker, and I was bound to have a breakdown sooner or later. Now I just needed to get back to Baker's place and apologize to him. Then I would tell him everything. No more running.

I pulled away from Wolfe. "Thank you," I whispered.

"Anytime." He leaned down and kissed my cheek. "Now go tell him the truth," he encouraged.

My phone buzzed from inside my pocket. I held up a finger at Wolfe while I pulled it out. I recognized the number as one of the lines from the doctor's office. Dread flooded through me. They wouldn't call so quickly unless they found something.

"Hello?" I said after I pressed the answer button.

"Miss Daniels, this is Marie from Doctor Hansen's office. We've gotten the results of your blood work and we need you to come in right away," she said.

I sucked in a breath. "I'll be there in a few minutes," I said, clicking off. I turned to Wolfe. "Can you take me to the doctor's?"

"I think Baker should take you, Rainey." He put his hands up defensively.

"There's no time. I need to get over there and figure out what the hell is going on," I protested. "Please, Wolfe."

He sighed. "Okay. Let's go." He grabbed his keys off the counter and led me out of the house.

I sat in silence while Wolfe drove me. A wave of nausea hit me and I had to take several deep breaths before I felt like I wouldn't puke. I closed my eyes and bit my lip, certain I was about to face my death.

"Rainey?" Wolfe asked. I opened my eyes and realized we were at the doctor's office and Wolfe was looking at me with a worried expression on his face. He must have called to me a few times.

"Here I go," I said with fake bravado.

I pulled open the door and Wolfe started to exit the truck, too.

"I need to do this alone," I said, putting my hand up, gesturing for him to stay. He nodded at me with understanding, although I could tell he wanted to be there for me. I needed to do this alone.

I walked up the three steps into the building and went to the receptionist's desk. She recognized me immediately.

"Miss Daniels! Come on in. We've got a room ready for you," she said, standing and opening the wooden door for me to go straight to the back.

The examining room was small and I sat in the chair next to the table, fear coursing through every bone in my body. They wouldn't have called me in unless things were worse, so at least I was prepared.

I didn't have to wait long, either.

"Lorraine," Doctor Hansen greeted me, a clipboard in hand. He closed the door behind him and took the rolling seat that was tucked under the computer desk in the room. He smiled at me and I was frozen in place. I gulped loudly and waited for him to tell me my fate.

"As I'm sure you can imagine, the leukemia is back," he explained. "The problem is that it's come back so fast, I'm doubtful more rounds of chemo will do much good. I want to stay positive, but I'm afraid that this time, the leukemia has come back fighting. Your body isn't going to be strong enough to handle the necessary treatments..."

He kept speaking but I was already checked out. He was giving me a death sentence. When the doctor didn't have much hope, it meant I was screwed.

"How long?" I interrupted him.

"Lorraine, there are some things we can do to prolong–"

"*How long?*" I asked a little more hysterically.

Doctor Hansen blew out a breath. "Three months."

My eyes widened and my hands were suddenly clammy. I gasped for air as his words registered. I felt like I was hyperventilating. Doctor Hansen handed me a brown paper bag from a cabinet in the room and instructed me to bend over and breathe into the bag. In a few minutes, I was calmer.

When I sat back up, Doctor Hansen looked at me sadly.

"There are things we can do," he said again.

"But all it would do is prolong it, right? And with chemo, I'd be sick," I replied.

"Yes. Chances are, you'd be too sick to do much of anything. But you could extend your life well into next year," he encouraged me.

"So, it's either three months of tiredness but being able to do what I want or several more months being permanently attached to an IV and being stuck in a hospital. Those are my options?"

Doctor Hansen looked at his clipboard. "Yes. I wish there was more we could do. I strongly suggest you get a second opinion, but I'm nearly positive the results will be the same."

"I'm going to forgo treatment, Doctor Hansen. If you have any meds that will help with pain at the end, I would appreciate it, but other than that, I'm not going to give up today when I have three months to live," I informed him. I would get a second opinion, like he suggested, but I doubted it would be different.

He didn't show surprise to my decision. Instead, he turned to the computer, typed out a few notes, and then turned to me. "I've sent a script over to the pharmacy for you. You can pick it up today. I would like you to come in once a week for checkups. Sometimes, we're wrong about the dates, but the only way to know for sure is to keep doing blood work and tests."

"I'll be sure to do that," I lied. If my time was up, either sooner or later, I didn't want to know.

Three months was hardly enough time to do the things I wanted to do. It was time to start living.

After more instructions from Doctor Hansen, I made my way out to Wolfe's truck. He raised his brow at me in question as soon as I was inside the cab.

"Everything's fine," I told him. "They thought they found something, but it turns out it was a fluke." I said it with a straight face and didn't even flinch over the lie.

Wolfe hugged me. "Great! When are you telling Baker?"

I laughed. "There's no need to tell him, now. I'm in the clear."

Wolfe pulled away from me, his emerald eyes narrowed at me. "You still need to tell him. What if it comes back in the future?"

"Don't get in the middle of this, Wolfe. I decide when and if I should tell him."

He didn't reply as he started the engine and put the truck in gear.

"Where to?" he asked.

"Baker's place, please. I've got to get the van," I instructed.

We drove in more silence, and although I was glad he bought my lie, I wasn't about to let anyone find out the truth. I needed to get the hell out of there.

It was a small town, and eventually someone would let it leak that I had leukemia. I didn't want to be around when it happened. Baker wouldn't understand why I never told him, and Mallory and Gabby would fret over me and treat me with kid gloves.

Wolfe dropped me off and I mentally made my plans.

Chapter Ten

Baker

I rubbed the back of my neck, anxious to hear from Rainey. I texted her a handful of times in the last two days with no response. She was ignoring me and I deserved it. I never should have treated her that way. She was the woman I'd grown to love, and I wasn't about to just lose her because I was an idiot. No matter how much I wanted to know what was up with her, I needed to be patient and wait for her to tell me. She was obviously dreading it, as was I. Something told me her news was going to change my life.

I picked up my cell, checking for the hundredth time to see if she texted me back and I somehow didn't hear it. No messages. I took a deep breath and set it back down on my desk. I made it to work without driving off the road, but only just barely. Once or twice, I had to swerve back between the yellow and white lines because I was about to go careening into a ditch. Driving distracted was *not* fun.

I made it, though. Going into the empty bar had been depressing, too. I tried not to think of the last few weeks I'd spent there with Rainey, the conversations we'd had, and how much I cared about her. The Landing was where I'd made a fool of myself that first night she'd come home over a month ago, and I couldn't imagine this place without her. Chances were, I screwed things up for us. I picked up my phone, typed out another apology, and pressed send before I could think twice. I shook my head at my own lack of willpower and then tossed the phone into the top drawer, hoping the whole *out of sight, out of mind* thing would work.

Jimmy appeared in the doorway. "Hey, boss, you got a minute?"

"Sure." I needed the distraction.

He came in and sat in the chair facing my desk. He fidgeted for a minute before taking a deep breath.

"What are your plans with the bar?" he blurted.

I blinked in surprise. "What do you mean?"

"Well, with Rainey gone, I wondered if you were going to abandon the bar to go after her," he explained.

"Wait, what? Rainey's gone? Gone where?"

"Oh, shit. I thought you knew. She flew back to LA yesterday morning. She didn't even tell anyone. Mallory only found out because she called Rainey's mom's house to get ahold of her."

He said it so casually, so matter-of-factly that I couldn't do more than stare at him. Which made him more nervous.

"So, I guess what I'm asking is whether you're going to leave us all high and dry or what? Because I'd like to buy you out."

"Buy me out?" I sounded like a dumbass, but things in my brain weren't computing properly.

"Yeah. If you're going to give up the bar, I'd like to buy you out and take over. I'm been doing a lot of research about it, and if you hadn't bought it when you did, I would have. I wish I'd gotten to it first, really. But I know what you have invested and the bank has approved me for a loan that would give you quite a bit more than what you've put in. The new deck adds a whole lot of value to the place and so they're willing to loan me more. You'd be set for a while. Here's my official offer." He slid a piece of paper toward me. "Think about it."

He left my office in a rush and I stared at the paper, not really seeing it. My mind was reeling over the fact that Rainey was gone. I pushed her so hard she left. It was as if she'd ripped my heart out and taken it with her. I leaned back in my chair and my whole body started to shake. I opened the top drawer and pulled out my phone with a trembling hand. I dialed the only person I could.

"Baker! Have you heard about Rainey?" Mallory answered on the first ring.

"Why didn't you tell me?" I demanded.

"I wanted to, Baker. Believe me, I begged her to tell you right away. But now the whole town knows and I think she left because she didn't want to deal with all the pity looks," she said.

"What are you talking about?" I clenched my fist around the phone. "The whole town knows about Rainey's secret – is that what you're saying?"

"Umm, yeah. You haven't heard?" Her voice was low and filled with concern.

"No, I haven't," I replied through gritted teeth. "Tell me."

"Let's meet for lunch, Baker. I want to tell you in person," she requested.

"Fine, meet me at The Wharf in fifteen minutes," I told her. I heard her start to argue but hung up.

I wanted nothing more than to fly out to LA and drag Rainey back to Maine, but I knew it would be pointless. She wasn't going to come back and be the subject of the town's gossip. If I was going to get her back, I was going to have to make a sacrifice for her.

Before I lost my gumption, I called Jimmy back into my office. It looked like I was about to sell my bar.

***

Twenty minutes later, I pulled into the parking lot of The Wharf. It didn't take me long to find Mallory.

"You're late," she admonished me.

"Bite me," I retorted. We sat at a picnic table on the upper deck. "So tell me."

Mallory swallowed and took a deep breath. "Rainey has leukemia."

I didn't reply or move, or even blink. I just stared at her.

"She found out a few years ago, when she moved to LA. The treatments she got seemed to work really well, though, and she's been doing pretty well since then. She lost a lot of weight, between the treatments and the actual leukemia, though, so she kind of stayed away as much as she could. She didn't want any of us here to be worried about her. Not even her mom knew about it. Her aunt helped her pay for the treatments and get her a job out there."

"When…when my dad died, Rainey came out to support me, but she was afraid to tell me anything because of Dad's cancer. She thought she was protecting me. Just like she thinks she's protecting you by not telling you. But the truth is, I think she's afraid of it. Wolfe told me that he took her to the doctor the other day to get the results of the blood tests she had done, because of all the bruising. He said she told him she was fine, but he didn't believe her. He told me that her smile didn't reach her eyes and he knew she was lying. And then the next day, she was gone."

Mallory looked at her hands.

"So she's dying, then," I finished for her.

"That's what we think," she admitted.

A vice gripped my heart as I thought about losing Rainey forever. I couldn't lose her, but more than that, I couldn't lose her without telling her how I felt about her.

"I'm going to LA," I informed Mallory.

"Are you going to bring her back?" She looked up at me, hopeful.

"Not if she doesn't want to. She deserves to be where she's comfortable, but I'm not going to let her pull away from me. I'm in love with her," I confessed, speaking the words aloud for the first time.

Mallory smiled at me. "She needs someone like you."

I didn't exactly feel worthy of Mallory's praise, but I took it anyway. I wouldn't let Rainey go through the pain without support.

"I need your help," I said.

"Anything."

"Well, I need to get to LA, but I'm also going to sell the bar to Jimmy," I started.

"Your bar manager? Wow, Baker. You are seriously in love with Rain, aren't you?" Her smile grew wider.

"I guess I am," I told her. "But I need someone to handle everything with the sale while I'm in LA. I'm not sure how long I'll be out there and I don't want to have to go back and forth with someone from the bank…"

"So you want me to take care of it? I'd be happy to help!" Mallory exclaimed. Her job at the bank was slightly different than what I wanted her to do, but I knew she wouldn't mind.

"Thank you. I need to get a ticket to LA," I said with trepidation. I didn't have any qualms with flying, but I was worried Rainey might reject me. No matter what, though, I was going to get the words said aloud to her and let her choose.

"Well get going! I'll handle everything with the bank," Mallory promised as she stood, rushing me. I stood in front of her and she hugged me. "Go get her, Baker. You two are meant to be together," she said with a smile.

I hugged her back and then drove home to pack and book a flight. I wanted to be in LA no later than tomorrow. I would win Rainey's heart if it killed me.

Chapter Eleven

Rainey

LA wasn't as glamorous as I remembered. In my head, it was pretty and sparkly, but in reality, it was crowded and hot, a little dirty, and void of emotion. In a sense, I wanted the emotional void, but it was still a lot to take in.

Of course, I was also facing a death sentence, which severely tarnished my perspective. Deciding not to get treatment had been a no-brainer, since it would only temporarily prolong a very sickly life. What I wanted was to enjoy what little time I had left.

Why I thought I belonged here, I'd never know. But I was here, which meant I was going to make the best of it. I glanced at my phone and ignored several texts from Baker, Luke, Mallory, and Gabby. There was even a stray message from Wolfe: *Are you okay?*

Since I didn't have any answers for anyone, I didn't reply. Texting back would lead to phone calls, and I couldn't handle that. I was a coward for my actions, I knew, but I couldn't help myself. I needed to get out, to get away. It was a harsh reality I was facing.

Death was hardly one of those things people thought about on a serious note until someone around them died, and I was dealing with my own mortality, which was far more intense. *Three months*, I thought. *Three more months to live.* It wasn't enough. There were still so many things I wanted to do with my life.

To distract myself on the plane to LA, I made a list of the things I wanted to do before I died. Then I threw it away when the drink cart came by and ordered a rum and cola. Even though alcohol usually made me sick, for whatever reason, it soothed my nerves on the plane. Then when I landed in LA, I spent several minutes in the airport bathroom, getting sick. Once I freshened up a bit, I met my aunt at baggage claim.

"Rainey!" she called, running toward me.

Brittney was my father's younger sister, and was very hip. Aside from the fact that she was only twelve years older than me, she was more like an older sister than an aunt. She supported all my decisions regarding the leukemia, even when they weren't the right decisions. Like keeping it a secret for so long. And not telling Baker.

I thought about texting him the truth, but I knew that was rude. I needed to call him, but I also needed to clear my head.

LA was full of life, even late at night when I arrived. It was well after dark and Brittney ushered me to her sporty car, refusing to let me carry any more than my purse. So I walked a few steps behind her and watched, bemused, as she awkwardly carried my suitcase and duffel. It was comical.

She tucked me into bed that night without so much as a question as to why I was back. I knew the morning would bring an inquisition, and it did.

Brittney grilled me with a hundred questions before I even had my first cup of coffee the next day. I answered her honestly, telling her about my death sentence. She pulled me close and squeezed me for several minutes. When she pulled away, there were tears in her eyes.

"I love you, kiddo," she said, addressing me like I was an eighteen-year-old kid again. I didn't mind. It was more of an endearment than a reference to my age.

"Love you, too. I just had to get away," I explained. My sudden appearance was not expected, but she took it all with a grain of salt.

"Of course. I took the day off work, so we can hang out together. I want your LA doctor to see you. I made an appointment for you and then we'll do something fun," she said excitedly.

I really wanted to be alone, but I couldn't tell her that. So I went along with her plans and we spent the day out and about. The doctor's visit was actually very routine, and not quite as heartbreaking as my visit to Doctor Hansen in Maine. I already knew what they were going to say before they said it, which made it only fractionally easier to deal with.

Brittney lived on the southern tip of LA, so we drove to the San Diego Zoo, my favorite place. It was nice to just forget the real world for a while and enjoy the animals. Once upon a time, I'd wanted to become a veterinarian. I always wanted to go to zoos, wherever I was, but there was only one in Maine and my mother never wanted to take me.

Mallory and I went to it when we were seventeen, but she'd been distracted by text messages from Luke, so she didn't really get lost in the animals like I did. My favorite exhibit was the Siberian tiger. They only had one, but she was gorgeous and I could stare at her for hours.

The San Diego zoo had several tigers of different breeds. I spent as much time as I could with the Siberians, but the white tigers were just as pretty. Brittney didn't talk much while we were at the zoo, but as soon as we were back in the car, she started up again. It was after five and I knew I should feel hungry. Instead, I felt nauseous. I rolled my window down a little as we got onto Route 5 North. The breeze helped calm my traitorous stomach.

I shuffled out answers to Brittney's questions, as much as I didn't want to, and she was appeased. When we got back to her house, I was tired from walking around so much and went to the guest room Britt set up for me. It was elegantly decorated, with a brightly colored flowery bedspread on the queen bed that matched the stenciling on the white walls. The night stand housed a small lamp for late-night reading, which I'd done a lot of over the years.

I lay on the bed, fully clothed and utterly exhausted, and promptly fell asleep.

* * * * *

I didn't wake up until after the sunrise, something that was gorgeous to watch if I was up early enough. I would have to set an alarm for tomorrow. Sunrise on the west coast wasn't as good as back east, but it was still beautiful. I stopped in the guest bathroom and then made my way downstairs to the kitchen. I needed coffee.

I thought about how much I missed Baker already. He had so quickly become a constant in my life. Leaving him had been difficult but necessary. Time apart would save him from any kind of heartbreak that would accompany my death. Putting that distance between us was my way of not getting too attached to him, I knew. Not that it mattered. I was already half in love with him. And his outburst the other day confirmed my suspicions about how he felt about me.

It wasn't enough, though. I was going to die and if we admitted our love to one another, it would only make the next few months harder to deal with. And after I was gone, he would have to deal with the pain every day, just like Mallory was doing. Watching her father die had broken her. She wasn't the same person anymore, and I didn't want my death to change Baker. He was funny and smart, outgoing, the life of the party. He deserved to be that way for the rest of his life, not to have his personality altered by the death of someone he loved.

I rubbed my eyes, willing myself to wake up; my body ached, my bones creaking in pain as I walked. I entered the kitchen without looking around, walking with tunnel-vision for the coffeepot, which was already brewed and deliciously hot. I grabbed a cup, poured some, and then added creamer before taking a sip and turning around to face Britt's dining room. My hip leaned against the counter while I grasped the cup in both hands and held it close to my nose, inhaling the sweet aroma.

When I looked up, I noticed two things. First, I wasn't alone in the kitchen. Second, the person in the kitchen with me was Baker. He was sitting on the far counter, his legs swinging back and forth as he waited for me to notice him. I took in the sight of him, memorizing every inch of him.

His feet were bare, as were his ankles and knees. He wore khaki shorts that hugged his hips but were lose around his thighs. His favorite light blue T-shirt adorned his torso; it clung to him, on the verge of being too small but actually fitting him perfectly. His hands rested on the edge of the counter and I could see the white of his knuckles as he gripped the counter, fighting for a casual appearance, but he was either nervous or angry. His dark sunglasses were pushed up over his head and rested in his cropped blonde hair, which was spiky and hot as hell. His eyes were pools of silver fire as he waited for me to speak. His lips pulled at the corners and I knew he was fighting a smile.

"What are you doing here?" I asked.

"I've always wanted to visit LA," he replied casually. He folded his hands in his lap. His smirk appeared and I felt my heart clench.

Perfectly white teeth reflected the light and my stomach hitched, causing a bout of nausea. I set my cup down as easily as I could and ran to the sink. I heaved several times and nothing came up, since I hadn't eaten in over twelve hours. Baker was at my side in an instant, gently pulling back my crazy bedhead hair and pulling several paper towels off the roll on the counter. He ran the water, wetted the towels, and pressed them to my forehead.

"You're burning up," he whispered.

I took several deep breaths before standing straight again. I had to be in control of myself before I did something stupid, like faint. I gripped the counter and slowly raised my body. Baker stayed close, his right arm around my waist and his left hand on my left shoulder. I turned to him even more slowly and met his eyes.

"You're so beautiful," he blurted. His eyes widened as soon as he said it. "Well, not like right now, you know, with nearly puking all over the place, but in general." He smiled wide.

"You're crazy," I whispered.

"Crazy about you," he retorted and leaned his forehead against mine.

I didn't fight him. My arms went around his waist and I moved my face away from his, scared to death my morning breath mixed with coffee and dry-heaving would repulse him. I rested my cheek on his shoulder and just held onto him. He was the support I needed more than anything in the world. When he was near me, I felt like I could overcome the looming darkness. I heard his sigh of contentment as his arms gathered me closer to him.

He lifted me up and set me on the counter, my thighs spread around his hips. He nuzzled my neck, his lips kissing my skin.

"I've missed you," he whispered against my throat.

I tilted my head to the side to give him better access and groaned. "Me too," I admitted, my fingernails digging into his back while he worked his magic on me.

I was lost to everything but the sight and feel of him against me. He smelled incredible, too. I inhaled his scent and let go of everything. All the stress that had been weighing me down was lifted, just by his presence.

His hands crept under my shirt and lifted it, exposing my breasts to his watchful gaze. I watched his gaze go dark as he spotted the bruise on my shoulder, but he didn't stop. He covered each breast with his hand and gently rubbed my distended nipples. I sucked in a breath, my earlier nausea gone as desire filled me.

I undid his belt and popped the button, slowly sliding the zipper down, reaching in his shorts and grasping him fully. I was rewarded with his harsh groan. He sucked on my neck more and dropped one of his hands to my panties. I was already wet and he groaned again when he felt it.

"I want you," he whispered against my ear, dragging my underwear to the side so he could touch me. He didn't waste any time with preliminaries; he thrust two fingers deep into me and I arched against him.

"Yes," I whispered back, lost to everything but him.

He yanked my shirt off and tossed it on the counter beside us, then pulled himself free of his shorts and boxers. He reached into his pocket and pulled out a condom, rolling it rolled on before I could do any more than stare at him. When he pressed himself against me, I scooted to the edge of the counter, anxious to get closer to him.

All thoughts fled, except for getting as much of him as I could. It didn't matter why he was here, or what he wanted from me; all that mattered was this – us. My breathing picked up again, and although I wasn't as limber as I would have liked, Baker did all the work and pushed into me, filling me so completely I cried out.

He stayed there for a moment, his eyes closed in ecstasy as he savored the feel of me. When his eyes opened, he looked at me intently and pulled out just a little. I instinctively brought my knees tighter around his hips, afraid he would leave me. His signature smirk greeted me and then he thrust in again. I threw my head back and his mouth came down to my neck again, suckling the sensitive skin.

"Rainey, is everything okay?" Brittney entered the kitchen and stopped short at the sight of us. My eyes flew to hers and she covered her mouth. "Sorry," she mumbled and fled the room. I heard the distinct click of her bedroom door down the hall and then I lost it.

I laughed so whole-heartedly that I hardly noticed Baker's horrified expression. He pulled completely out of me, ripped off the condom, and tossed it in the trash behind him.

"Tell me I'm not standing here in your aunt's house with my dick out," he grit out. He gently tucked himself back into his pants while I let out all my pent-up laughter. He tried to look at me seriously but eventually broke out in a grin.

"I blame you for this," he accused.

"Me? I was just itching for some coffee when you attacked me with your hot body and devilish smile," I defended.

His lips parted at my words, his pupils dilated. He had an incredibly hungry, sexy look on his face. I was almost drawn in again as he moved toward me.

"No!" I playfully slapped him away. "I am horrified that Britt just found us like that." I jumped down from the counter, grabbing my shirt and slipping it on. "I have to go get dressed. Try to keep it in your pants, okay?"

"Hurry back, or I might attack your aunt with this thing." He wiggled, thrusting his crotch out at me. "It's got a mind of its own!"

I made my way up the stairs with a chuckle, unable to get the picture of Baker waving himself in front of me. Regardless of how much I might have believed he and I should stay away from each other,

I was glad he came. I hurried into my room once I cleared the stairs. Even though I knew he would never make a move on my aunt, I didn't want to leave the two of them together alone for too long.

Chapter Twelve

Baker

I shook my head in disbelief over my own behavior. I was there to reprimand her, to demand to know why she left and to make her feel guilty. Instead, I tried to jump her at first sight. It was as if not seeing her for three days ruined me. I wanted nothing more than to be with her as much as I could for the rest of our lives. Granted, I knew hers wouldn't be much longer, but I still wanted every moment, every smile.

"Are you decent?" came a voice from the hallway.

I stifled a laugh. "Yes, ma'am."

"Good," she said as she came around the corner into the kitchen. "Let's have a chat, shall we?" She sat at the dining room table and I meekly followed.

"I know we met earlier, but maybe I wasn't clear before. Rainey is not to be hassled or attacked, even if she wants it. I won't have my niece put under undue stress," Brittney addressed me.

She was only a few years older than me, but she scolded me like a child. When I showed up at seven that morning, I had explained who I was and she welcomed me into her home. She let me know that Rainey was still asleep and that I could hang out until she woke up. Then Brittney went into her room and left me alone.

I had wandered the living room, smiling at the number of pictures of Rainey and Brittney together. They always looked happy together, which was nice to see. I knew Rainey's mom was hardly a good role model. Maybe being in LA had been best for her.

When I heard Rainey's door open, I hid in the living room and waited for her to turn her back. Then I jumped up on the counter and waited for her to notice me. It had been fun. I never suspected it would escalate so quickly, though.

"Do you understand me?" Brittney asked when I didn't answer her fast enough.

"Yes, ma'am. I apologize for what you walked in on, and I take full responsibility for it," I told her.

"Don't be so dramatic, Baker," Rainey said from the stairs as she walked down. "We're both adults and we don't need to apologize for anything." She glared at her aunt.

I had to bite my tongue in order not to laugh, but then I noticed what Rainey wore. If I thought she was adorable in an oversized tee, she was absolutely stunning in a pair of short jean shorts and a tiny pink tank top. Her long legs were bare, but tan. Long, dangly earrings hung from her ears and she'd even put on some lip gloss. I tried not smile.

"Don't talk to your aunt that way, Rain," I admonished her. "She's just looking out for you."

"Exactly. Thank you, Christopher." Brittney smiled at me. I winced at her use of my full name. No one ever called me Chris anymore, let alone *Christopher*. I let it slide, though.

We both turned to Rainey, who had picked up her forgotten coffee cup. "Okay, I'm sorry! Geez, you act like you never did anything when you were young." Rainey rolled her eyes.

Brittney shook her head. "I did. But now, I have to get to work. Try not to get her pregnant, okay?" She looked at me and I went into a coughing fit to hide my laughter. The woman was a force to be reckoned with. I now knew where Rainey got it from.

She stood, blew Rainey a kiss, and was out the door before I could say goodbye. Once I heard her car pull out of the driveway, I turned to Rainey, who stood against the counter looking sexy and edible.

"Don't even think about it," she warned when I moved to get up. "You stay away from me until you explain what the hell you're doing here."

I sighed. "I came to see you. I wanted to ask you why you left."

"You ever hear of this new invention called the telephone? Apparently, you can talk to people thousands of miles away without jumping on a plane to see them in person." She glared at me.

"Oh, right, because you answered every single one of my texts," I ground out through clenched teeth.

She had the decency to flinch at my words. "You're right. I'm sorry. Do you want some coffee?"

I nodded. She brought me a cup and sat in the chair her aunt had been sitting in. "I'm sorry, Baker. I know I should have told you, should have said goodbye, but I just couldn't do it," she rushed out.

"Why did you leave?"

105

"I don't know." She abandoned her coffee and stood up, waving her hands around while she spoke. "I was afraid if you knew the truth, you'd leave me, so I left first. And then I got the news that I only have a few months left – it's like a damn death sentence. Leukemia is hardly something I ever wanted to deal with, but the treatments were working! I was better. And then the bruises started again, along with fevers and night sweats... I was scared," she finished, looking at her hands, standing in the middle of the kitchen.

I had to turn around to follow her movements with my eyes. She paced while she talked and when she finally stopped, I stood.

"It's okay to be scared," I said, walking over to her in the middle of the kitchen. "Hell, it's not even happening to me and I'm scared."

"Really?" She looked up at me with tear-filled eyes.

"Of course. It's not every day I fall in love with a woman who's dying," I joked half-heartedly, taking her hands in mine.

"You're really in love with me? I mean, you said so back in your apartment, but I kind of thought it was just the heat of the moment."

"I said it before? I don't even remember that. But I will remember this. I love you, Lorraine Daniels."

She gulped. "You shouldn't love me, Baker. I'm no good for you."

"What are you talking about? You're the only woman who can stand my quirky sense of humor." I smiled at her, trying to hide my disappointment that she didn't say it back. She wasn't ready, and I promised myself I would be patient.

"I'm going to *die*." Her voice broke, and along with it, my heart. "If you love me now, you'll just be heartbroken later, and you'll be alone."

"I've been alone before, Rainey. While you were in LA, I spent several years trying to find happiness, using women like playthings to fill a void in my soul. But it was you – you are the only one who can fill that void. When you came back, I knew right away that you were it for me. And knowing that you have a shelf life," I paused, waiting for her smile, "well, that just means that I'm not going to let you go again. Not if I can help it. If I had the choice of a hundred healthy years to live or twelve short weeks with you, I'd choose you, every single time."

I leaned forward and kissed her sweetly. Tears escaped her eyes and I wiped them away with the pad of my thumb. She smiled sadly at me again.

"When did you get so sweet?"

"I've always been sweet. You just never noticed me. In fact, you pushed me away then, just like you're doing now. But let's get one thing straight." I leaned down to look her in the eye. "I. Am. Not. Going. Anywhere." I gave her a quick peck and then went back to the table, picking up my coffee and heading into the living room to look at photographs again.

She didn't move for almost a full minute as my words settled over her. I tried not to grin as I eyed all the photos again. When she finally moved, she came into the living to look at pictures with me.

"This one was taken at the airport, right after I moved here." She pointed to a frame that sat on a shelf about shoulder height.

I took in the photo, memorizing every detail. *This* was the Rainey I remembered. She was tall, with shorter blonde hair and those same fiery green eyes.

The only thing different was her size. In the photo, her hips were fuller, rounder, but still delectable. Even her breasts were plumper, filling the tattered T-shirt she wore more fully. She looked like a kid, and in many ways, she was. I turned to look at her next to me.

She had changed over the years – her slimmer waist, longer hair, even the way she dressed was more refined, older. But she was still there, the Rainey I loved. The girl who laughed at my stupid jokes and shook her head at me when I was being an idiot. Just *Rainey*.

I was lucky to have her in my life, and although I regretted not having her in my life for the last few years, I wanted to make up for lost time in the next few months. I wanted to be by her side when she breathed her last, knowing that we had made the most out of our time together.

"So what do you want to do today?" I asked her.

She glanced at me, her surprise evident in her raised brow.

"How long are you staying?" She asked.

"For however long you are," I informed her.

"What? You can't stay here." She stepped away from me.

"I can pretty much do what I want. Free country, and all that. But I am staying here because I love you and I'm not about to let one moment pass without spending it with you," I explained.

"But… What about when I die?" She looked down at her hands.

I put my finger under her chin to get her to look at me. "Then a little piece of me will die, too. Until then, I want to enjoy being with you."

I saw the fear creep into her eyes and knew I scared her, but I needed her to know I wasn't about to walk away.

And then something else appeared in her bright eyes. Something akin to mischief.

"What are you thinking?"

"Well, on the plane ride here, I made up a bucket list…"

"Hell yes. Whatever's on it, we'll do," I promised.

"I sort of threw it away." She looked sheepish.

"We'll write a new one, then. No big deal. What's the first thing that comes to mind to do?" I asked her, ready for anything she could think of.

"How about Vegas?"

I wasn't ready for that.

Chapter Thirteen

Rainey

Vegas wasn't actually on my original to-do list. It had been on my mind, though. Living out west as I had for several years, I always wanted to do something reckless and frivolous. But the leukemia had made me more reserved, less likely to do something just for the sake of doing it. I always told myself that *someday* I would get to Vegas, do all the things I wanted to do.

Someday was now. With only a few months to enjoy my life, if I wanted to do something, I needed to do it right away. Once I got to a certain point, I would have to be hospitalized, or at least have a home nurse. Until then, I wanted to get as much out of this life as I could. And that meant letting Baker in and taking a chance.

"Vegas?"

"Yeah. I always wanted to go, but money has always been tight for me, paying for treatments and whatnot. So I want to go, you know, before *I* go," I grinned.

"Well then, hell yeah! Let's go." He pulled me into a hug and lifted me up, swinging me around the living room. I laughed with him, unable to do anything to stop my growing feelings for him. He was perfect for me, exactly what I needed at this point in my life.

"I have to pack," I told him and he put me down.

"My bags are already in the rental car. I'll just watch you pack," he suggested, taking my hand and leading my up the stairs.

He pushed open my bedroom door and flung himself sideways on my bed. He picked up a magazine I left on my nightstand and flipped through it, hardly paying me any attention. I stood there, staring at him like a fool for several minutes.

"What are you doing?" He finally looked up at me. "Get packing!" He cracked an invisible whip at me and made a *whippish* sound. Then he turned back to the article he was reading. A man who read magazine articles. Insane.

I turned away from him and pulled my duffel out of the closet. I packed jeans, shorts, tanks, and tees. I threw in a few pairs of socks, and then eyed Baker nervously before pulling open the drawer where I kept all my lingerie. Many of the items inside were see-through, lacy pieces that revealed more than they covered, but something told me Baker would appreciate them.

His attention was focused solely on the magazine so I stuffed several teddies into my bag, along with the matching panties. He would definitely appreciate my effort. I pulled out a pair of jeans and laid them on top of the delicates, just in case he decided to look up. I went into the guest bathroom and grabbed my straightener, body wash, shampoo, and conditioner. I set everything on the end of the bed and then picked up my travel makeup bag out of the closet. I placed all my hair stuff into it, running back to the bathroom for bobby pins, my hair brush, and anti-frizz serum. Once I had everything set, I moved on to shoes.

When I left LA for Maine last month, I left most of my designer shoes with Brittney, since there weren't many places to wear four-inch heels in Maine. Vegas, however, was a different story. I could easily get away with heels there; plus, Baker was way taller than me, so I wouldn't tower over him. It was win-win. I picked four pairs, figuring that any more wouldn't be necessary and any less would cause me serious problems when dressing myself while we were there. I carefully placed them in the duffel bag, making sure the heels wouldn't snag any of the teddies.

Baker turned to me as I zipped up the duffel. "Ready?"

"Almost. I just have to go through a few more things," I told him.

"Okay, well I'm going to go make the reservation. Come downstairs when you're ready." He tossed the magazine back on my night stand and got up. He planted a quick kiss against my lips and then waltzed out of my room without a glance back at me.

I stared after him for a full thirty seconds before I shook myself. I needed to pack at least one sexy dress. Maybe two. I turned to the closet and realized my wardrobe was hardly acceptable. I flipped through each dress, discarding it for one reason or another. I was dissatisfied with every dress I owned. All I wanted was something black, sleek, and clingy.

The ones in my closet were flowy and vibrant. I sighed.

Maybe Aunt Brittney would have something along the lines of what I wanted. *Aunt Britt!* I needed to call her and let her know that Baker and I were taking off. I pulled out my cell and dialed her work number.

"This is Brittney," she answered.

"Hey, Britt. It's Rainey."

"I figured you and Baker would be hot and heavy by now," she laughed.

I shook my head. "No, not exactly. He actually wants to take me to Las Vegas," I started. "He asked me what I wanted to do, kind of like a bucket list, and I've always wanted to do Vegas."

"That sounds great! Have fun, kiddo! You'll be back in what – a week?"

"Yeah, I think so. Hey, can I borrow a black cocktail dress for the trip?" I asked hopefully.

"Of course. Go raid my closet! Lord knows I won't be needing them any time soon." She emitted another laugh and then turned serious. "Are you safe with him, Rainey? If something happens, will he be able to take care of you?"

I thought about it for a second. "Oh, yeah. He was handling me with kid-gloves before he even knew about the leukemia. I would say it's going to be a mellow time in Vegas. And I trust him," I told her.

"Good for you. Don't let him go, girl. Not many men would stick around and watch you fade out of their life. But anyway," she said with a lighter tone. "Have a great weekend and shoot me a text or two while you're gone so I know you're okay. Love you!"

"I will. And I love you, too, Britt," I told her. I clicked off and tucked my phone back in my pocket, then hefted my duffel over my shoulder and picked up my makeup bag off the bed. I made my way downstairs and noticed through a window that Baker was outside on the small front porch, on his phone. I dropped my bags by the door and went into my aunt's bedroom.

It was a first-floor master suite, with an amazing master bath. The décor was bright, just like the guest room. I pulled open the door to her walk-in closet and just stood there, staring at the wide array of clothes encased inside. She was one of those women who bought clothes and then never wore them. From the doorway, I could count at least ten articles of clothing with tags on them. And that was just what I could see. I entered the closet and moved to the back, where she kept her dresses.

Britt's OCD meant that all her clothes were put into sections by the piece of clothing and then further organized by color. She had no less than twenty black dresses, and they were ordered alphabetically by designer. It was sickening and amazing, all at the same time. I went through each dress individually, analyzing them one-by-one, trying to decide which one would drive Baker the craziest.

When I came across one that had a low scoop-neck line to show off plenty of cleavage and a short hem, I knew I'd found the one. The shoulder straps were about two inches wide, which would leave my arms bare. It was perfect. I gingerly pulled the tag out and realized there was still a price tag on it. I almost didn't want to look, didn't want to see how much money Britt paid for this scrap of cloth.

My curiosity won out, though. I flipped the price tag over and sucked in a breath. *Three hundred forty-*

nine dollars. It was insane to pay that much for a dress, but if I knew Aunt Britt, she would want me to take it anyway. Like she said, she didn't wear cocktail dresses much anymore. Her VP status at her job meant she didn't schmooze the clients; she paid people to do that. So I went to the very back of her enormous closet and found a black garment bag to hide the dress in. I gently put the dress inside after removing the tag and carried the bag over my shoulder as I walked into the living room.

Baker stood there waiting for me by the front door and I noticed my duffel and makeup bags were already gone.

"I put your stuff in the car. And we're all set with a hotel." He grinned at me, gesturing to take the garment bag.

I gave him a stern look as I handed it over. "No peeking," I warned.

"Oh, something good, then. Maybe just a little glance?" He playfully moved his hand toward the zipper.

"No!" I slapped his hand away from the zipper and took the bag back. "I'll just carry it. Are we ready?"

"Yeah. Do you need to leave a note for your aunt or something?"

"I called her. So we are all set," I confirmed.

Baker led me out of the house and waited patiently while I locked the front door behind us. I turned to look at his car for the first time and had to laugh.

"A sports car, really?" I exaggerated a sigh.

"What? It's fast. We'll get to Vegas in no time," he promised with a glance at his watch. "I say we make it in less than three hours."

"Three hours? Do you have a fever?" I reached up and put the back of my hand against his forehead. "Even in zero traffic, it's a four-hour trip."

"How would you know? You've never been," he taunted.

"Touché."

"Just get in the car and let me drive. Three hours," he predicted again. I laughed, turning back to the car.

It was a bright red Challenger, brand new. The leather seats were cozy and surprisingly cool. Baker must have started it while I was inside. He opened up the trunk to put my garment bag in the back.

"I'll put it in the back seat," I told him.

He nodded and pushed the trunk lid closed. I tucked the bag behind my seat and let it rest on the hook near the roof of the car. I sat on the cool leather and adjusted my shorts before turning back to Baker just as he climbed into the driver's seat.

It was like watching a clown try to fit himself into a clown car. At six-three, Baker was hardly a little guy. Add to that his bulging muscles, and watching him get in was comical. I covered my mouth to stifle a laugh.

"Something funny?" he asked once he was inside.

His eyes met mine and I felt the heat rise between us. "Not a thing," I whispered.

He slammed his door closed and then leaned over to me. "I have to tell you something," he said in a serious tone. Baker was usually so playful and full of jokes, I was actually scared when he stared intently into my eyes.

"Yes?" I answered with baited breath.

"You are so fucking hot," he said, snagging his hand behind my head and bringing me close to him so he could kiss me.

It was a hot, searing kiss and I knew I was much too close to the flames. By the end of this, I was going to get burned. But I couldn't find the will to pull away. Instead, I put both my hands on his chest, in an effort to bring him closer or push him away, I don't know. His tongue sought entrance into my mouth and I opened for him, eating up every hot touch. His hand on my neck rubbed encouragingly and I moaned into his kiss.

He ended it long before I wanted him to, and we were both out of breath. "Hot damn," he whispered against my lips.

I laughed, this time actually pushing him away. "Let's get going," I suggested.

He seemed to be in a hurry as he pulled away. He strapped his seatbelt on while I put mine on and then turned the key. A loud, grinding noise emitted from the car and I had to hold back my laughter as I realized the car was already running.

"Damn thing," he mumbled and then shifted into gear. He looked at me. "Not one word."

Then he gunned it and we were off to Vegas.

Chapter Fourteen

Baker

I thought for sure we would make it to Vegas by noon, but traffic was much worse than I anticipated. The trip took almost five hours and Rainey was driving me crazy. She didn't do or say anything upsetting, but those short shorts were distracting as hell, and it was more than once that I had to grip the steering wheel with both hands to get focused on the road.

But we did get to Vegas. Eventually. Even with her long legs calling to me. We hit the strip and she lit up. It was early afternoon, so it wasn't as dramatic as coming in at night, but Rainey was still animated as she eyed all the casinos and show places. Her smile was wide and I knew this was a great idea. She deserved to feel some happiness before she started to deteriorate.

When she turned that amazing smile to me, my gut clenched. "This is amazing, Baker."

"Yeah, amazing," I agreed, but I stared directly at her, letting her know I thought *she* was amazing. I didn't care about Vegas, but seeing her, all smiles and truly enjoying herself, made me happy. I was so in love with her. There was no mountain I wouldn't move to make her smile.

She blushed and turned away, getting my meaning. She looked out at our surroundings and when I pulled into Caesar's Palace, she turned her wide eyes back to me.

"*This* is where we're staying?" she asked, incredulous.

I grinned and pulled up the valet. "Yes, ma'am."

I popped the trunk, got out, and tossed the keys to the young guy waiting nearby. I slipped him a ten-dollar bill and then walked around the car. A bellhop opened the door for Rainey and she sat there, still amazed. I directed the bellhop to our bags, including the garment bag behind Rainey's seat, then walked over to where she was still rooted in the passenger seat and tugged on her hand.

"Come on." I helped her up. "Lots more to see."

She walked forward with me, still in shock. We entered the lobby and the architecture was stunning. I'd never been to Vegas, either, but I figured we should go in style. I wanted this to be the best time of her life. I led her over to the check-in desk.

"Welcome to the Palace. Checking in?" the young woman at the counter asked us.

"Yes, we have a reservation under Christopher Baker," I explained.

The woman's eyes lit up. "Yes, Mr. Baker. Your suite is ready for you. Here is your key, and if you need anything at all, please just dial zero and we'll be happy to help you with anything at all." She handed me a set of keys. "You will need to go all the way to the end of that hallway." She pointed toward the far end of the lobby. "There's an elevator and you'll have to use your key to get to your floor."

I thanked her and led Rainey down the narrow corridor.

She looked nervous as we walked, hand-in-hand. I stuck one of the keys into the slot at the elevator and the doors opened for us.

"This is surreal," she finally said when the elevator doors closed behind us. I smiled down at her.

"It's pretty cool, if you ask me. Although," I said, looking down at my belt, "I'm not getting a sig on my beeper."

She burst into laughter. Quoting one of the movies we watched together in our early days of sleeping together was a perfect icebreaker.

"Promise me I won't have to come find you on the roof tomorrow, okay?"

"Nope. I can't make that kind of promise. But I'll tell you what – if I end up on the roof, you will be right there with me and we will get crispy in the sun together." I grinned.

She shook her head and the elevator stopped, the doors opening into a small foyer with a single door. We stepped off and walked to the door.

I held up the key to our room. "Ready?"

She nodded.

I slipped the key into the slot and pushed open the door. I let Rainey go in first, knowing she would be shocked.

Aside from several columns in the space, the suite was wide and open, with floor-to-ceiling windows that gave a great view of the city, even in the daytime. There was a circular couch in the center of the room that faced the window, as well as an extra-large flat-screen television on the far wall. The flooring was granite, as were the countertops in the kitchen. A stocked full bar graced the kitchen, along with a complete set of dishes and cookware, not that we would be doing any cooking.

My plan was to keep Rainey busy in the casinos until late at night so that when we got back to the room, she was exhausted. As much as I wanted her, I didn't want to take the chance of hurting her again. The memory of bruises along her body tormented me. I didn't want to be the one causing them. And aside from my slip that morning in her aunt's kitchen, I had been able to keep my hands off her. Mostly.

That kiss in the car before we left was pretty hot. I felt myself get hard just thinking about all the things I wanted to do to her. I closed my eyes and took a deep breath. I needed to gain some control. When I opened my eyes again, Rainey was standing in front of me, just staring at me.

"Hey, stud." She licked her lips provocatively, running her fingers across my shoulders, causing the skin under my T-shirt to ripple. I wanted her so damn much.

"Hey, yourself," I said as casually as I could.

"This is a great suite," she said. "Should we check out the bedroom?"

Rainey grabbed my hand and led me to the corner of the suite, opened up an extra-large door, and we both stopped, stunned by the room. Aside from its enormous size, the best part of the room was the monster of a bed that sat in the center. It was a four-post, king-size bed decorated all in white. It was a symbol of purity, to be sure. But more than that, the white down comforter was covered in fresh rose petals.

"What the hell…" Rainey turned to accuse me.

I shrugged. "It's the honeymoon suite."

"*Honeymoon?*" she squeaked

"Oh, relax. I knew it would be a nice room, and I wanted you to have a good time." I grinned at her.

"Well, I *do* plan to have a good time," she whispered, pressing herself against me.

I groaned in satisfaction, the feel of her breasts against my chest driving me crazy. The woman was an enigma.

***

Hours later, the bed was a mess and we were both hot and sweaty. Not that it wasn't awesome. Rainey was insatiable. With every touch, every tender kiss, she demanded more. It was hard to keep my control with her. I tried not to hurt her, but I had a feeling I would be kicking myself later when I saw the new bruises. And they would appear; there was no doubt in my mind.

I lay on my back, staring up at the mirrored ceiling, something we hadn't noticed until we got into the bed. It made for some interesting positions, that was for sure. A fit of giggles beside caused me to turn to Rainey. I turned on my side and propped up my arm on the pillow, resting my cheek against my fist.

"What's so funny?" I demanded.

"Look at yourself," she suggested.

I glanced down and realized I was covered in red and white rose petals. Each delicate piece was stuck to the sweat that still clung to my body. There were three on my torso and several hanging precariously off the only part of my body that extended.

Surprisingly, knowing she was looking at that part of me caused me to want her again. I wasn't sure how much more I could take, but I wanted her.

"Baker...?" She lifted her beautiful green eyes to mine and raised a brow.

"Ready for round four?" I asked.

"No! No more," she squealed and tried to get out of the bed. I flung an arm around her waist and dragged her back to the plush mattress, hefting myself above her.

"This is my domain," I said with a scowl. "And I will have you."

She erupted in more giggles and then managed to buck me off her. I wasn't expecting her to push me, so I ended up on my ass on the floor. I sat there, staring at her as she peeked at me above the comforter.

"Apparently, it's not your domain as much as you thought," she teased.

I growled and moved to get up. She was off the bed before I could catch her and she ran to the bathroom. I was one step behind her, and when she stepped into the shower stall, I knew she had nowhere to run. Instead of covering herself and hiding, though, she surprised me. She turned on the water, got the temperature just right, and then turned on the showerheads, one on each side of the stall. She crooked her finger at me and then ran her hands down her body, the water creating beautiful imagery for my growing erection.

"Get in here," she muttered when I didn't move.

I grinned and went after her, pinning her gently against the wall and kissing her passionately. I didn't let up on my assault, either. Her blonde hair was wet in my hands and I held her still for my kiss. She squirmed but seemed to enjoy herself.

"I've never had sex in the shower," she admitted when I finally let her breathe.

I felt myself grow harder at that.

"First times are my specialty," I said, referencing the fact that I took her virginity years ago.

And just like that, we were *both* ready for round four.

Chapter Fifteen

Rainey

Sex in a shower was a new experience, but I quickly learned that no matter how much stamina I thought I had, Baker had more. The man was a sexual beast! If I even hinted at sex, he was ready. It was enlightening and oh, so sexy.

After our romp in the bathroom, I pleaded with Baker to leave me alone in the amazing shower for just a few minutes. He hesitantly agreed with the promise that we would have more shower fun tomorrow. I asked him to bring my bags into the bathroom, too, which he did without a complaint.

With soaking wet hair, I wrapped a towel around my body and used a hand towel to wipe away some of the fog from the mirror. I clicked on the hair dryer attached to the wall and waved it over the mirror, watching as the fog cleared. Once I could see myself, I flipped my head upside-down and turned the dryer to my hair. I ran my fingers through my hair to help the process, but it took *forever*. Once it was mostly dry, I shut it off and stared at myself in the mirror. There was still a slight fog, but I noticed a few bruises right away.

Baker was going to flip. Luckily for me, they were all in places my dress for the night would hide. I smiled in anticipation. Baker was in for a real treat. I pulled out my makeup, deciding not to wear too much. There were a few love bites on my neck that needed covering, but other than that, I only applied eyeliner and mascara, going for a more natural look. The dress was going to overpower any makeup I could put on, anyway.

I plugged in my curling iron and waited impatiently for it to heat up. Once it was hot, I curled strands of my hair around it, just to give it a wavy look instead of curly-cues. When I was satisfied with how it looked, I unplugged the iron, blowing out a breath as I shed the plush white towel. Even after all these years, I never got used to seeing myself as a thin person.

I knew I was, of course. It was just hard to see myself other than the plump high school girl I'd always been. And I'd never felt as comfortable in my own skin as I did when I was with Baker. He made all self-consciousness disappear when he worshipped my body. His tender loving of me was no different than when we were kids, either. He had adored my curves then, when I was chunky. He gave me courage to appreciate my body. It was his blatant sexuality and confidence in himself that would have given me hope for a future.

If only...

But I refused to think about it. Baker and I agreed on the trip to Vegas that we wouldn't discuss my leukemia or the future. We both wanted to just forget the world and enjoy the right now. So that's what we did. *Four times.* How on earth the man could keep it up so often was beyond me. Not that I was complaining. He was like a sexual hero. My own personal sex ninja.

I smiled at the thought and unzipped the garment bag Baker had carried in and set on the hook on the back of the bathroom door. I pulled the sleek black dress out and gingerly stepped into it. There was a zipper on the side and as I pulled it up, I tried to not feel exposed. The dress was probably normal on my five-foot-five aunt, but I had at least four inches on her, most of which was torso. The hem barely came to mid-thigh. If I bent over, the world would see all my business. I would have to remember that, in case I dropped anything tonight.

As revealing as it was, it fit perfectly. A short line of cleavage was visible above the neckline – enough to be sexy but not so much as to be slutty. It was like the dress was made for me. I opened my duffel and found the black heels I had packed, setting them on the floor. They were open-toed, so my bright pink toenails would stand out against the dark color. With a little trepidation, I opened the bathroom door and stepped into the bedroom, ready for Baker's taunts.

To my surprise, the room was empty. The bed had been roughly made, too, which I found absolutely endearing. Few men would have taken the time for such a menial task. I strutted across the floor, my heels clicking all the way as I made my way to the in-room bar. Baker was behind it, pouring drinks. My heart stopped for the barest of seconds at the sight of him.

Gone was the casual, redneck-ish guy from Casper, Maine. This new Chris Baker could give Brad Pitt a run for his money. His blonde hair was gelled and spiky, his eyes vibrant, but it was his attire that caused me pulmonary stress. He wore a charcoal gray, pinstriped three-piece suit that matched his eyes perfectly. The button-up shirt underneath was crisp and brilliantly white. A gray-and-white striped tie hung off the collar, loosened but sexy as hell. He glanced up at me and I think my stupid stare was mirrored in his eyes.

We stood there, less than ten feet apart, staring at one another for probably an entire minute. "You look amazing," he finally spoke.

"Ditto," I replied, still unsure if I could formulate a full sentence.

His eyes dilated as he eyed my bare legs. He gulped. "I'm making myself a drink. Do you want something?"

Nausea spread through me. "I'll just have some water."

"You okay?"

"Oh, yeah. Just no alcohol." I gave him a smile. I walked over and accepted the bottled water he held out to me, giving him a quick peck on the cheek, and then pulled away. "So what's on the agenda tonight?"

"It would seem we were both thinking that tonight would be a bit fancy," he gestured to our attire, "so I think we'll head out to a nice, romantic dinner and then walk the strip a bit to see which casinos we want to bet in."

"Sounds good," I said. "Are you ready?"

"Yeah, but first, I want to show you something." He turned off the lights and for the first time, I realized that the windows were covered. The room was immersed in darkness.

I wasn't afraid of the dark or anything, but when Baker's hand brushed mine, I jumped a little.

"Easy," he whispered, his mouth close to my ear. "Come with me."

I gripped his hand like a vice. "Don't let me fall," I begged.

"Never."

A shiver went down my spine as I considered his words. I knew, without a single doubt, that Baker would always be there to catch me if I ever did fall. I blinked away the tears that formed as I thought about how little time we had together. When we reached the window, Baker let go of my hand to pull on the string and spread the curtains covering the window.

It was only just after seven in the evening, but the sight I was presented with was breathtaking. The sun was low in the horizon, mixing with the vibrant blue and purple of the darkening sky to form a hazy pink sunset that was absolutely stunning. I stepped closer to the window, putting my hand on the thick glass, wistful for as many sunsets as I could take in. Baker stepped up behind me and wrapped his arms around my waist,

I held on to his arms, clutching him to me. He was, in every sense of the word, my rock. In the short time we'd been *dating*, Baker had become so important to me. I leaned into him, both literally and figuratively. He held me tight and I was comforted by his presence. At that moment, I realized there was no place on earth I'd rather be than with him, no one else I'd rather spend my last few months of life with. I could spend my last days doing something as crazy as going to Vegas, but it was only going to make me happy spending that time with him.

I turned to face him, searching his silver eyes with mine. "I love you," I blurted.

His eyes went wide, his skin pale. For a second, I wondered if it was too much for him. But true to his nature, Baker plastered on his signature grin and winked at me.

"I love you, too," he pledged. He tipped his head toward me and pressed his lips to mine. His touch ignited a fire within me and I wrapped my arms around his neck. "Easy," he said again with a laugh. "We have plenty of time for that later. But if we don't leave right now, we're going to miss our reservation, and *that* would be a shame."

He disentangled himself from my grasp, tightened his tie, and grabbed my hand to lead me back to the elevator outside our suite. The elevator ride was spent with me standing there, looking flushed and on fire while his thumb rubbed soothing circles across the top of my hand. Even when we weren't speaking, he was comforting me.

By the time we reached the lobby, I was a mess, sighing almost continuously. This was the perfect getaway for us, no matter what came later. We would face our future, or lack thereof, with dignity and trust in each other. Love was going to change us both completely.

Chapter Sixteen

Baker

Hearing the words I longed to be spoken from her lips surprised me, but even further, filled me with a sense of completion. It felt like I'd waited so long to hear her tell me she loved me, and then when she did, it was every bit as amazing as I imagined it would be. From the look of surprise on her face after she said it, I guessed she hadn't intended to say the words aloud.

That was fine with me, though. She did say them, and I wasn't about to let her forget. I knew I never would. As much as I loved her, it was a little more difficult to figure out why she loved me. I was just an average guy who fell in love with the perfect girl next door. And logic screamed at me that she wasn't perfect. No one was. But Rainey was about as perfect *for me* as a woman could get. She tolerated, maybe even understood, my deranged sense of humor, had a laid-back attitude toward life, and was one hell of a girlfriend.

She's dying. I shook the negativity away, knowing that dwelling on the fact that she was going to die would only drown my happiness. I wanted to just enjoy our time together. However long we had left.

We walked out of the hotel and out onto the strip. Her eyes lit up like a little kid when she realized all the lights were starting to glow. The brightness was nearly blinding, but we managed. I clasped her hand in mine with no intention of letting go. No matter where this night led, she was going to stay by my side all night. I planned to soak up every moment with her.

"So what's for dinner?" she asked as we walked along the sidewalk.

"The Bellagio," I answered.

"Oh! Do I get to order the most expensive thing on the menu? You know, since this is like a real date?"

I looked at her sternly. "I expect you to eat your weight in food."

She burst into laughter. "I might just do that. I'm famished from all the activity this afternoon."

I just grinned at her, knowing we would be repeating the events of this afternoon again when we got back to the hotel. But food was definitely on the list things that had to happen first. And I'd heard nothing but good things about the Bellagio. Plus, the casino was right there, so we could gamble a little.

My phone buzzed in the pocket of my designer trousers and I groaned. I wanted nothing more than to ignore it, but if it was Mallory, I knew I had to answer.

"Sorry," I told Rainey as I slid my thumb across the screen of my cell. "Hello?"

"Dude! Where the hell are you?" Luke's voice yelled in my ear. I glanced at the screen again. He was calling from Mallory's cell. I would have to kill her.

"What do you want?" I barked.

"Where are you?" he asked again.

"Vegas."

"What are you doing in Vegas?"

"What are you, my mother? I'm here with Rainey and we're on a date, so unless you have something important to say, I am going to hang up in five seconds. Five…"

"Umm, Mallory said you were going to bring Rainey home – are you?" he tried.

"…Four…"

"Did you really sell the bar?"

"…Three…"

"Are you going to move to LA permanently?"

"…Two…"

"Are you in love with her? Mal said you were but I don't believe it-"

"…One… Bye, Luke."

"Wait! Will you answer my damn question?" he screamed in my ear. I had to pull the phone away from my head.

"Not unless she wants to. Yes. If I have to. And abso-fucking-lutely I love her. Goodbye, Luke." I pressed the end button, effectively cutting off whatever he might have said in reply.

I had unknowingly stopped on the sidewalk and Rainey stared up at me with amusement in her eyes. "What's so funny?"

Her smile widened. "Well, the phrase 'abso-fucking-lutely I love her' is a pretty awesome thing to hear. I can assume you're talking about me…" She wanted to hear the words again, so I decided to torment her.

"Actually, I was referring to my *other* girlfriend," I teased.

She slapped my shoulder with her free hand. I was still clinging tightly to her left hand. I looked down at our entwined fingers and raised them to my lips, gently kissing each of her fingers.

"You, Rainey. Only you," I said in between kisses. She blushed at my words and tried to escape my grasp, but I wouldn't let her. Instead, I laughed, tucked my cell back into my pocket after switching it to silent, and then tugged her along the sidewalk toward our dinner date. Rainey giggled while her face turned red, but she followed along.

Dinner was more than filling, and we both ordered more food than we could possibly consume. She still had room for dessert, a feat that I admired her for. I hated when women suppressed their appetites to appeal to a man. Rainey made good on her promise to eat her weight in food. Then she devoured most of a fudge brownie sundae, hardly leaving me any at all.

"You ready to do some betting?" I asked once the last plate was cleared and the waiter left our bill on the table. I didn't want to look at it, but I was pleasantly surprised that it was under two hundred bucks. I thought for sure we would have spent more than that easily. I pulled three hundreds out of my wallet and left them on the table.

I helped Rainey out of her chair as she stared at the bills. "When did you become Daddy Warbucks?" she asked incredulously.

"I have to keep my money situation under wraps. Otherwise, the ladies would be all over me." I winked at her.

"I can imagine. Having a sugar-daddy at my disposal is pretty interesting."

We laughed and made our way to the lines of tables. "So what's your game?"

"I'm not sure. I've never really gambled before," she admitted.

"Okay, how about we start with some slots, then?"

She nodded and we wandered around for several minutes before a slot machine caught her eye. She started to open the small clutch purse she carried with her but I stopped her. I shoved a hundred dollar bill into the machine before she could protest and sat next to her, throwing a twenty into the machine. I wasn't too interested in gambling, but watching her was just as satisfying.

Her eyes lit up as I explained how to choose the number of lines and bet per line. We went through a couple bucks as she figured it out, and once she did, she was off, bouncing up and down on the seat every time she won the slightest amount. I set my machine to the minimum bet and then hit the rebet button every once in a while, just so I could occupy the machine. When a waitress came by and asked us if we wanted a drink, I requested a whiskey and cola.

I didn't want to get drunk, knowing as I did that Rainey couldn't drink, but a little buzz would loosen me up. Especially if we hit any of the clubs on the strip and she wanted me to dance. I knew better than to think that my dance moves rivaled Channing Tatum, but I could throw down, if I needed to. The problem was, I lacked the courage, and no one had seen me dance. *Ever.*

But if Rainey asked, I would agree, no matter what my reservations were. For the time being, though, she was content to spend money in the slots.

After an hour of play, she lost quite a bit but then managed to get herself ahead of the game. When she had two hundred bucks sitting in the machine, I leaned over and kissed her cheek.

"Let's try one of the table games," I suggested.

"Okay," she replied, breathless in her excitement. "Which game?"

"Blackjack is the easiest to learn," I informed her. I showed her which button to press to cash out and she took her printed ticket to the cash machine. I followed closely behind her, enjoying the view.

"Stop staring at my ass," she reprimanded me once she had a wad of twenties in her hand and we were walking toward the game tables.

"I can't help it," I admitted. "It's amazing."

She laughed and we found two seats open at a blackjack table near the edge of the room. We sat and she traded her money in for chips. She bet like someone who had no idea what she was doing, and within minutes, she was broke.

"Damn!" she groaned, getting up from the table. "How do people count cards? I could barely keep track of the ones he dealt to me, let alone everyone else's."

I followed her, carrying my drink in my left hand and dropping my free hand to the small of her back. I guided her through the now much more crowded space and she turned to talk to me, her voice an octave louder than normal so I could hear her.

"Where to next?"

"Anywhere you want," I promised her.

She seemed to think about it for a moment and then an evil smile crossed her lips and I knew I was in trouble. When she leaned close to my ear to tell me her suggestion, I swallowed hard.

"Let's go to a nightclub!"

Chapter Seventeen

Rainey

The first club was filled with about a million sweaty people and we quickly ducked out, moving on to another. The second one had more of a laid-back feel, definitely more my style. The music was loud, though, and I pulled a hesitant Baker onto the floor. He moved gracefully, but without much enthusiasm. He complained over and over that he was hot.

"Go give your jacket to the coat check!" I suggested over and over.

After about the fourth time, he finally sighed in defeat and left me on the dance floor, pulling off his jacket as he went. I danced by myself for all of ninety seconds, and thankfully, no one tried to join me. When Baker returned, he'd rolled up his sleeves, loosened his tie, and looked extra sexy. Some pop culture hit blared through the speakers and pounded out a rhythm and I pulled Baker to me by his tie as he approached. I figured I would just dance around him a little, maybe get him fired up, and then we would leave and return the hotel.

What I wasn't prepared for was Baker. His dance moves looked like they were taken straight out of a recent male stripper movie. His body matched the beat perfectly and he rubbed himself against me in perfect unison with the thumping bass. I turned and ground my ass into him a bit and he replied in kind. I could feel his hardness pressed against me, and it was more than exciting. His hands gripped my hips to keep our bodies together and I threw my hands up in an attempt to be sexy.

I should never try to be sexy.

I smacked him in the face with my left hand then when I turned around to apologize, the heel of my traitorous shoes dug into his foot and he howled in pain.

"Shit! Sorry!" I yelped, truly mortified.

When he lifted his foot to his hands and jumped around for a full minute, hopping on one foot while he held the other, I lost it. Laughter bubbled up out of my throat and I could do nothing to contain it. He glared at me, but I was helpless. He made his way to an empty barstool and I followed him, both hands covering my mouth to hide my giggles.

Even after he sat, he held on to his foot with both hands and I stood nearby, helpless to do anything but laugh at him.

"It's not funny," he growled.

"Oh, are you super grumpy now? Will you be able to make it back to the hotel?"

"Not sure," he mumbled as he pulled off his shoe and sock to examine his foot.

A bright red welt was already forming on his skin and I immediately felt guilty. I hadn't thought it was that bad, but seeing it was a reality check.

"I'll go call us a cab," I said with a pat on his back. I turned away but he grabbed my hand and pulled me into his lap.

He growled again, a trait I was beginning to find endearing, then put his lips on mine. Passion roared between us, in the midst of the crowd around us, and by the time he lifted his head, my hands were molded to his neck, clinging to him for dear life.

"Go get a cab," he ordered.

I almost reminded him that I had been about to do just that, but instead, I stood up, straightened my dress, and left him there.

Outside the club, there were people everywhere. It was after ten and the strip was full. Getting a cab was not going to be an easy task. I went to the curb and put my hand out, just like I'd watched people do on TV for years. Not a single cab stopped. I sighed.

When I felt heavy hands on my hips, my first thought was that Baker had limped his way outside to help me hail a cab. No such luck.

"Hey, baby, how much for the whole night?" a deep voice boomed behind me. I turned around and looked up at the man before me.

He wasn't gross, per se, but he was definitely dirty. His hands on my waist were covered in filth and he was missing one of his front teeth.

"You couldn't afford me," I said and immediately regretted it. I wasn't in Maine, where an advance at the bar could be pushed away and there were plenty of good Samaritans to help. People here in Vegas probably wouldn't help unless I screamed rape. And even then it was iffy. I tried to push his hands away from me, but his grip tightened and I was stuck in his grasp.

"You whores are all the same. Think you're too good for a paying customer. Maybe I'll just take the goods for free," he threatened.

Just as panic set in, a hand landed on the creep's shoulder and he whirled around to face his attacker, my protector. Baker's eyes were engulfed in silver flames and his face was flushed in anger. He swung a punch at the guy's face and then lifted him up by his neck. No small feat, considering the guy was beefy and at least an inch taller than Baker.

"You touch her again and you're dead," he promised before he tossed the guy to the ground. His body hit the pavement with a loud thud and he groaned. Baker met my eyes. "You okay?"

I nodded, still a little shaky from the encounter.

"Let's get out of here," he suggested and I agreed. He tossed an arm across my shoulders and we walked several yards away from the scene. He managed to get us a cab and we climbed in the backseat, where I got as close to him as I could.

"What were you thinking?" he accused as soon as he was comfortable.

"Me? You're the one who punched that guy!"

"I'd do it again if anyone dared to touch you," he vowed.

"You were just jealous," I joked, desperate to lighten the mood.

Baker turned his unusually serious gray eyes toward me. "It wasn't jealousy, Rain. It was fear. If I hadn't come out when I did, what would have happened to you?"

It was a question I didn't want to answer. "I know. I'm sorry."

"It wasn't your fault."

And I knew he was right, but I couldn't help but look at my outfit and wonder if my attempt to push

Baker over the edge was actually a little incriminating. I looked like a high-priced call-girl, no matter what Baker thought. I sighed and hung my head, shamed.

Baker shucked a finger under my chin and forced me to look up at him. "I love you."

I never tired of hearing him say it. "I love you, too."

He smiled and kissed me gingerly. He entwined his fingers with mine and I rested my head on his shoulder, utterly content.

When the cab stopped in front of the hotel, Baker paid the driver and then hobbled out and into the lobby. Just before he reached the glass doors, he whirled around to face me.

"You know what I want?" he asked, his eyes back to his playful self.

I thought about it for a second. "Tacos?"

"Hmm, not a bad suggestion. But what I *really* want…is to marry you."

I stared at him, unmoving, shocked, and completely frozen in place. I searched his eyes, desperate to find a hint of amusement in them. I found none.

"Are you serious?"

"This wasn't how I wanted to do it. I have a ring," he mumbled. *A ring!?* "And I planned to do it tomorrow morning at breakfast. But I love you, Rainey. No woman will ever compare. You're it for me."

I gulped.

"I know it's sudden and probably just a tad bit crazy," he limped forward to take my hands, "but I want you to be my wife." He awkwardly knelt down on one knee and pulled a little black box out his pocket. He flipped open the box and the diamonds glinted in the bright lights. "Marry me."

It wasn't a question so much as a demand. Chris Baker wanted to marry me. Even though I was dying. Even though he would have to live his life as a widower. Even though –

"Stop thinking, Rainey and just *feel*. What does your heart tell you?"

"Yes," I said before I could think too much.

He slipped the silver band onto the ring finger of my left hand, kissed it, and then stood, gathering me in his arms. He spun around, his damaged foot forgotten as we both laughed with glee. I was giddy.

"I love you," he finally whispered into my ear when we came to a stop.

"I love you," I replied as I looked around. People around us were snapping photos on their camera phones and I realized that Baker would want to remember this moment.

I asked a beautiful Asian couple to take a few pictures for us, showing them how to use my cell phone camera. Baker and I posed ridiculously for at least a dozen photos. I figured we were bound to like one of them. I took my phone back from them eventually and thanked them profusely. They congratulated us.

We walked hand-in-hand to the elevator to our room. Once the doors slid closed, Baker pressed me up against the wall, pressing kisses down my throat. I moaned in delight and then groaned in frustration when the doors opened much too quickly on our floor.

We entered the suite and I half-expected him to jump me as soon as we were behind the closed door. Instead, he poured two glasses of champagne.

"Champagne upsets my stomach," I confessed as I took the goblet from him.

"I guess it's a good thing its sparkling grape juice, then." He kissed my forehead and we sat on the couch, snuggled together. "A toast," he lifted his glass, "to the most beautiful woman in Vegas agreeing to marry me."

I clinked my glass against his and took a sip, the bubbles tickling my lips. Doubt settled in at that exactly moment and I thought about the repercussions of my actions. Whether he accepted it or not, I was going to die. That meant he was going to come to terms with my illness, even though we agreed not to discuss it.

"We need to talk." I set my glass down on the coffee table and tucked my feet beneath me. Baker's arm was resting along the back of the couch and his fingers played absently with my hair.

He sighed. "Already? Can't we just enjoy it?"

"I know you hate to be serious, but this is important. I can't marry you unless you promise me something."

"An ultimatum already?" He set his glass next to mine. "Lay it on me."

"After I'm gone," I started. Baker made a movement to interrupt me but I stopped him. "No, let me finish. After I'm gone, and you've had time to grieve, I want you to promise me that you'll find someone who makes you happy."

"What? That's insane," he argued.

"I know it seems weird, but, Baker, you were made to live a long, happy life with someone, not to be a widower your whole life. I understand why you want to marry me – believe me, I get it. And I love you for it. But if we're going to do this, then I want to know, beyond a shadow of a doubt, that you will move on someday and allow yourself to love someone else. I need to know that you'll be happy."

"I am happy," he started.

"You know what I mean. You deserve to be in a committed, long-term relationship where you are loved every day for the rest of your life."

"I have you, Rainey."

"Not for long. My time is limited. And although I will love you forever, the truth is, I won't be around forever. I won't marry you unless you promise me," I confirmed, sticking to my convictions about it.

He seemed to realize that I didn't want the easy answer. He sat back on the couch, pulled his arm away from me, and looked at his hands. He fiddled his fingers together for a moment before he answered me. When his eyes came back to mine, they were misty.

"I've never felt this way before. Hell, I don't think I've ever been in love at all. And if this is your requirement for marriage, then I can't do anything but agree. I don't like it. But I'll do it. After you're…" he struggled to find the right word. "…*gone*, I will, at some point in my life, move on and love someone else. But let's get one thing straight." His eyes bore into mine. "I will *never, ever* stop loving you. As long as there's air in my lungs, you will forever be in my heart, the completion of my soul."

I gave him a little smile through the tears that had already formed. "I love you."

His reply was to pull me in for a kiss.

Chapter Eighteen

Baker

I lost my mind.

That was my only thought when I woke up, slumped over on the couch hours later. Rainey was nowhere to be found and I didn't go looking for her right away. I needed some time to think. Marriage wasn't a problem. I wanted her to be my wife more than anything in this world.

The more I thought about her demands, though, the more nervous I got. I had been holding out for a new treatment or miraculous healing, but the cold, hard truth was that Rainey *would* die. Whether I wanted to deal with it or not, facts were facts. I picked up a glass of leftover juice and took a swig, not caring about the fact that it was old. I needed to appease my overly dry mouth. I swallowed the now flat liquid and took deep breaths, determined to calm my anxious heart.

I loved Rainey. Logically, I knew I didn't need to worry about anything more than that. She was the only person in the world I would fight for, and even though the ending of this fight was predetermined, I still wanted to win. I wanted to save her, to be her knight in shining armor. If only things were that simple.

Marriage was the one option I thought for sure she would refuse. And for a minute, it looked like she would. But then she threw caution to the wind and accepted me. It was liberating. I wanted nothing more than to prove my devotion to her for the rest of my life, whether she lived or not.

Her demand that I find love again after she passed was insane. I agreed to placate her, but there was no one my heart would survive this plague. I was already half brokenhearted *now*, what was going to happen in a few months when I couldn't look at or be with her at all?

I sucked in a breath, but didn't feel the air rush into my lungs. All I felt was despair at the thought of never being able to see her again.

I leaned forward and hung my head between my knees, drawing gasping breaths. It took a full minute before I calmed down enough to lift my head. When I did, Rainey was standing in front of me looking sleepy and so sexy.

"You okay?"

"Yeah, I'm fine," I assured her. I stood and walked over to her, wrapping my arms around her in a hug.

"Still want to marry me?" she asked with a glint in her eyes.

"Abso-fucking-lutely."

She grinned, her teeth glinting in the light coming from the strip. "That's good to know," she said, turning in my arms to lean her back against my chest with my arms still around her.

I leaned down to kiss her neck, softly inhaling her sweet scent.

"So when do you want to marry me?" I asked her softly.

"Oh, I don't know. How about next year?"

I squeezed her a little to let her know I didn't appreciate the joke.

"I was actually thinking we should do it in Maine," she answered.

"Are you sure? That means flying out there, you know," I teased, knowing how much she hated to fly.

"I'm sure."

"Next week?" I suggested.

She gulped. "I think that would be perfect." Her voice quavered a bit but she kept her smile frozen in place.

"Don't be afraid," I whispered in her ear.

She turned in my arms, lifting her hands to the back of my neck. "I'll never be afraid of you," she promised.

I kissed her but pulled away before I could enjoy it too much.

"I'm starving," I admitted with a smirk.

"Does this place have food?"

I barked with laughter. "*Does this place have food* – that's like asking if the place has air!"

She stuck her tongue out at me and then moved away toward the window to watch the city below us. "Make us something, then," she demanded.

I gave her ass a playful slap and was rewarded with her yelp of surprise. I winked at her and went into the kitchen to search for food.

When I returned to the living area a few minutes later, Rainey was sitting on the couch, very quiet and almost nervous. I set down a tray of food for us to share and her eyes widened.

"You still eat Doritos and Skittles?" She stared up at me in shock.

"Some things are too good to leave in childhood," I replied, plucking a handful of chips from the bag and tearing open one of the small bags of fruity goodness.

I popped a chip and several pieces of candy into my mouth all at once, chewing loudly just to annoy her. "This is me, babe. Maybe *you* should be the one rethinking this marriage thing."

She seemed to ponder my words, and my gut clenched in anxious anticipation. Fear flooded me and I stopped breathing, afraid she would admit to not wanting to marry me after all. But then she laughed and swiped the bag of Skittles off my lap.

"You'll be a diabetic with all this junk food," she said, even as popped a few Skittles into her mouth.

"Look who's talking," I admonished, giving her a glare. "Besides, life doesn't get much better than chips and candy with the girl I love."

Her emerald eyes turned watery and she looked wistful. There were circles under her eyes and I realized that being up this late wasn't good for her condition.

"Let's go to bed," I suggested as I stood. I held my hand out to her.

"Sounds like a plan," she said seductively.

By the time we walked into the bedroom, though, she was half-asleep already and I had to lift her into the bed. I laid her on the mattress and she mumbled in her near-sleep state.

"I love you, Baker," she whispered and then rolled over, snuggling under the thick covers. I stood there smiling like a fool at her for several minutes, just watching her sleep.

When I turned away, I had a big smile on my face and I *knew*, without any doubt, that loving Rainey now would be worth whatever heartache came later. I went out into the living area, picked up the tray of food, and took it to the kitchen. I noticed my phone blinking when I passed where I had set it on the coffee table, so I picked it up on my way to clean up.

There were four missed calls from Mallory and I assumed they were from Luke, but I listened to the voicemail anyway, just in case.

"Hey, man. What the hell is going on? You and Rainey just disappear and now we're all worried about you two! Call me back," Luke pleaded. I rolled my eyes and pressed the button to delete the message.

There were several text messages and I scrolled through them.

I typed out a quick reply to Jimmy, who asked about how to close out the bar sales for the day on the main computer.

Two messages were from Mallory's cell and a quick glance told me they were really from Luke. *Where the hell is his phone?* I sighed and sent a quick reply telling him that everything was fine and Rainey and I would be back in Casper next week. I didn't tell him why, though. I figured Rainey would want to tell her friends herself.

A text from Gabby asking about my whereabouts and mostly giving me hell for up and leaving town like a jerk made me feel like a small child being reprimanded by his mother. I sent her a message, too, promising to have Rainey call her tomorrow and explain everything.

Wolfe even texted me, although his message had nothing to do with my whereabouts and everything to do with alcohol. *What's the best mixer to go with spiced rum?* I laughed softly to myself and answered him. Leave it to Wolfe to not even acknowledge my disappearance and act like I'd been there the whole time.

It was nice to hear from everyone, though, as much as I didn't want to admit it because they were mostly annoying. They all cared about Rainey and me and this was just their way of showing it.

My phone rang in my hand before I could put it down and I sighed again. The caller id showed it was Mallory and I hoped it would be.

"Hello?"

"Baker! Where the hell are you?" Mallory's voice rang out through the line.

I grinned. "Didn't Luke tell you?"

"He said you were in Vegas. That's not true, is it?"

"Of course it is," I assured her. "We are having a great time, too."

"Let me talk to Rainey," she demanded.

"She's asleep. It's like two in the morning here, Mal," I informed her.

"Oh. Right. Well, have her call me *as soon as she wakes up*. No excuses."

"Yes ma'am. I'll have her call you," I promised.

"Good. Now tell me something," she started.

"What's that?"

"Are you really bringing her home?"

"The short answer is yes. I don't know for how long, though. It might be just a short visit," I told her, aware of every word I spoke so that I didn't give away too much information.

Mallory breathed a sigh of relief. "Good. I need to see my best friend and give her hell."

"No giving her hell, Mal. She's been through enough," I chastised her. "I mean it. Just let her do things her way."

"But —"

"We all supported you when you went through something tragic. Now it's your turn to return the favor."

Silence.

"Did you hear me?"

"Yeah, I heard you," she huffed. "I'll keep my mouth shut. I don't *want* to, but I will. She deserves it, I guess."

"Good. Now I'm going to bed. I'll have her call you tomorrow," I promised again. We said goodbye and clicked off.

When I went back into the bedroom, Rainey was snoring softly. I jostled her a bit when I climbed in next to her.

"Everything okay?" she mumbled as I put my arms around her.

"Everything's perfect," I assured her with a quick kiss.

We fell asleep and for one night, I felt like everything *was* perfect in our world.

Chapter Nineteen

Rainey

It was hard to enjoy our week in Vegas, knowing as I did that there were a million things to be done before the wedding. Baker and I booked a flight that would land in Portland, Maine, on Wednesday, with the wedding scheduled for Saturday. Four days were hardly long enough to plan the event, but Gabby and Mallory took on a bunch of responsibilities for me, for which I was grateful.

I was so worked up for the wedding that the flight home barely bothered me. I was too excited.

The Portland International Jetport was relatively empty when we arrived, but everyone waited for us at baggage claim. Mallory, Luke, Gabby, Ember, and even Wolfe all gave us a round of hugs and congrats.

The boys, it seemed, were going to throw Baker a bachelor party tonight so he wouldn't be hung over on Saturday. I appreciated the sentiment. My sister and two best friends were going to be my bridesmaids and I couldn't be happier. The girls and

I were going to head over to the bridal shop and see what was in stock. Buying off the rack didn't even bother me, knowing that I would get to marry the man of my dreams.

I barely had time to give Baker a quick kiss before Mallory, Gabby, and Ember pulled me away, demanding all my attention. Before I was taken away, though, he managed to slip a credit card in my hand.

"Buy everything you want. Make this your perfect wedding," he whispered in my ear. My fingers wrapped around the plastic and I smiled at him.

I had money, of course; hell, Aunt Brittney had given me several thousand dollars, cash, before we got on the plane in LA, demanding to be a part of the wedding. She even claimed that I was like a daughter to her. She would be flying to Maine on Friday.

I took Baker's credit card with the knowledge that I probably wouldn't need it, but it was nice to have, just in case. The girls pulled me toward the car, carrying my bags for me and chatting incessantly about the wedding.

"So, we were thinking that we could do it in the backyard of my dad's place," Mallory said. Even though she and Luke were living in it now, she still referred to it as her dad's. She was adorable.

"That sounds great!" I gushed, truly excited about my big day.

We piled into Mallory's car and continued to discuss the wedding while Mallory drove us to the bridal shop nearby.

"So what are you thinking for a dress?" Gabby asked from the backseat.

I turned to face her. "I'm hoping for something flowy and maybe a halter top…"

"Sounds good to me. I can't wait to see you in a white dress!"

I smiled at her and Mallory weaved in and out of traffic, unusually quiet.

"What's wrong, Mal?"

"I was just thinking about how I wished our dads could be here," she whispered, tears forming in her eyes.

"Me, too," Ember said from the back seat.

"They'll be watching over us," I told them. I turned to Gabby again. "Speaking of dads... Since mine can't be here, I was kind of thinking of asking Wolfe to walk me down the aisle."

"What? Why not Luke? You guys are way closer," Gabby replied.

"I know. But Luke is the best man. And believe it or not, Wolfe helped me realize how much I loved Baker. He gave me a very fatherly speech before I left for LA."

"And then you immediately ran away to LA. Must have been some speech," Gabby scoffed. She rolled her eyes and crossed her arms over her chest.

"I know you guys have your issues, Gab, but this is important to me. I don't have my dad to walk with me, and I don't want to walk alone. Please don't fight this," I begged.

"Fine. Do what you want. But if this is some ploy to try to get us back together, Rainey, I'll kill you," she threatened. And then a light when off in her head, like she only just realized what she said. "Ohmygosh! I'm so sorry, Rain. I didn't even think before I –"

"Don't apologize! I don't want to be treated with kid gloves. And I can honestly say that trying to get you and Wolfe back together never even crossed my

157

mind. So you can relax. And I'll make sure the two of you don't sit together at the wedding."

She seemed to calm down after that and Mallory parked the car in the mall lot nearest to the shop. We walked into the shop and the place was filled with bridezillas yelling and demanding unheard of things from their bridesmaids. We were taken to a changing room surrounded with mirrors and I explained what kind of dress that I wanted, and that I needed to buy off the rack. The woman helping us was helpful and listened intently to what I wanted before taking off into the abyss of white gowns.

She returned with four dresses, all likely candidates for my wedding, and I began to try them on. Mallory, Gabby, and Ember pulled up a few chairs outside the dressing room and nodded or shook their heads each time I came out to show off the next selection. When I came out in dress number four, they all were motionless.

"What do you think?" I tried to engage them, but they were speechless. The dressing room itself didn't have any mirrors, so I turned to face the plethora of rooms covered in mirrors and joined them in stunned silence.

This was the one. It fit perfectly, clinging beautifully to my thin body. The halter top was intricately embroidered with dozens of tiny white flowers. The neckline was modest without being old fashioned and the skirt flowed simply, the small train hardly dragging at all. It was a gorgeous dress.

"You look amazing, Rain," Mallory said finally, the first to speak.

"I don't think you need to try on any more of them," Gabby agreed.

Ember had tears in her eyes. "You're beautiful."

I looked at the sales woman standing nearby. "I'll take it."

* * * * *

With my dress tucked safely in the backseat of Mallory's car, we decided to hit up the department stores for their bridesmaid dresses. I didn't want them spending a fortune, and there were some cute ones.

We settled on a pale pink dress with a knee-length hemline. It was available in each of their sizes, so we considered that a sign. We put their dresses next to mine and then drove home to Casper, an hour-long trip filled with chats about everything to do with the wedding.

We dropped the dresses and my bags off at Mallory's house, deciding the boys could stay at Wolfe's farm house for the duration. Baker and I already agreed we wouldn't sleep together again until we were married, a feat that was difficult in Vegas, but we both knew it would be worth it.

"Okay, so I called Sally's and they said they could come up with a few arrangements for us to take a look at this afternoon," Mallory said.

"Oh, what kinds of flowers do you want, Rainey?" Gabby asked me as we all took a seat in Mallory's living room.

"I don't even care, honestly. The only thing that matters is marrying Baker. Everything else is unimportant."

"That means we get to influence her, girls," Gabby whispered conspiratorially.

I shook my head at the three of them. They continued to discuss flowers for half an hour before they dragged me to the flower shop. We poured over arrangements and colors for three hours before everyone agreed that we had the perfect arrangement. My bouquet would be ready Saturday morning, along with the girl's mini-bouquets.

It was after five by the time we made it back to Mallory's house.

"I need food!" I demanded.

"We were hoping you would say that." Mallory grinned sheepishly.

"What?"

"We planned a little bachelorette party for you," Gabby admitted.

"You guys! You didn't have to do that. It's not like I can get drunk or anything."

"That's true. But we thought you might enjoy a stripper!" Mallory announced.

My face flushed at the thought and I was mortified. "No way! I would have to be drunk to deal with a stripper!"

Mallory and Gabby burst into giggles. "We figured as much," Gabby finally explained. "How about a day at the spa?"

"Oh, that sounds like fun," I agreed.

"Let's go!" Mallory led the way to her car, which I belatedly noticed was already packed with several bags. They had loaded up the car and I didn't even notice.

"You kind of dozed off before your demands for food," Mallory informed me when I looked at the bags in surprise. "We took advantage. But for now, we're heading to the hotel to check in and you get a full day of relaxation tomorrow."

I was more that excited. I needed some pampering.

The hotel was one I'd never been to, but had often fantasized about staying at. The pillows were plush, the room huge. It wasn't Caesar's Palace, but it came close, in my eyes. Plus, I would get to explore the spa at this place.

"Your first appointment is tonight at seven," Mallory filled me in once we were all checked in and sitting around the hotel room. "You've got a massage scheduled."

I squealed in delight and hugged her. "You guys are the best friends a girl could ask for."

"Well, if you're going to get married, you should do it right." Gabby smiled wistfully.

"Oh, Gabs, I'm so sorry about you and Wolfe. I know this must be hard on you."

"No, it's okay," she assured me. "I'm just a little nostalgic. My and Wolfe's wedding was hardly more than a two-minute thing at the courthouse. Maybe that should have been clue number one for me," she laughed.

"The size of the wedding doesn't matter, you know," Mallory said suddenly, sitting up straight in her spot on the couch. "It's all about love. Big or small, a wedding is about dedication to one another, for as long as you live."

I agreed with Mallory whole-heartedly, but I knew Gabby would disagree. She and Wolfe had been through some tough times over the years, and her impending divorce must be driving her crazy. Having Mallory spout off about the sanctity of marriage was probably the last thing she wanted to hear.

"Sometimes things fall apart. Dreams die," Gabby whispered.

Mallory moved closer to her and took her hand. "Then you've got to find the glue to put them back together, or discover a new dream together. Dreams come and go, but love is forever."

I wiped the tears away from my eyes at her words, knowing in my heart that her words were just applicable to my life as Gabby's. I needed to let go of my broken dreams and just love Baker as long as I was able.

Mallory's speech enlightened my situation and I realized I had less than an hour before my appointment. I told the girls to order room service and then I went about finding some paper and a pen, ready to write my vows to Baker.

Chapter Twenty

Baker

The bachelor party was actually very mild, considering I spent the last four days in Vegas. There were no brawls or fights, but there were definitely shots. A bottle of Jagermeister was passed around between the three of us and we enjoyed Jagerbombs throughout the night. When darkness fell, we took to the streets of the Old Port, bar hopping all night to celebrate my upcoming nuptials. We stopped in at a sports pub that was far less crowded than other bars and took a table.

We ordered some appetizers and beer. Luke was surprisingly quiet. "What's up with you?" I asked him, snagging a tortilla chip and scooping some salsa onto it.

"Well, I was going to propose to Mallory this week," he admitted.

I choked on the chip and Wolfe had to pound me on the back before I could breathe again. "What do you mean you were going to propose? You never told me that!"

"I know. Joe left me a family ring, though, and even gave me his blessing, in the form of a letter. I've been holding onto it, carrying it everywhere with me, but the timing hasn't been right. But I finally decided to do it this week, on Friday night, and then you guys had to plan your wedding this week." He sounded defeated.

"So do it anyway," Wolfe suggested.

"I couldn't do that. Rainey would have a fit," Luke argued.

"Actually, I think it would be perfect. If you do it at our reception, all your closest friends will be there. Rainey would love it," I promised, only a tic nervous that she wouldn't like the idea. But I felt like I knew her well enough to say she would enjoy it.

"If you're sure," Luke hedged.

"Absolutely."

"Do it!" Wolfe raised his beer and we clinked the bottles together.

Hours later, we were too drunk to stay out any longer. We took a cab to our hotel in downtown Portland and rode up to the fourth floor. We were in our room for less than ten seconds before we all passed out.

The next morning, I woke up on the floor with an extreme headache, but I made it to the bathroom before I blew chunks. I splashed water on my face afterward, taking note of the way my stomach felt and tucking the information away for future reference. I'd never been so drunk in my whole life. No one should ever consume that much liquor.

I wiped my face with a hand towel and went out into the room, collapsing into a chair by the window. Luke was face-down on one of the beds and Wolfe occupied the other. They were both still fully clothed and I stifled a laugh until I realized I was wearing my clothes from last night, too. I swiped my phone off the table and decided to text my fiancée.

Good morning, Beautiful.

Hey babe. The girls are treating me to a spa day. How was your night?

I looked around the room, noting the beer bottles and half-full cups of Jager.

Fantastic.

I bet. Are you going to pick up a tux today?

Yeah, I'll text you when we get back into town. I love you.

I love you, too. See you later.

I smiled. It was like once she let her guard down, she was this whole other person, one not afraid to be close to someone else and let them in. It was a good change of pace.

I wondered what would have happened if I had gone after her to LA all those years ago, when she left after high school. As much as I wanted to say we would end up right where we were today, I knew I couldn't be sure. Rainey had been different then: self-conscious, shy, and about to face the biggest challenge of her life, her leukemia. Everything I loved about her was due to the fact that she had changed over the years; she'd grown up. Who could say that we would have stayed together if we had gotten together back then?

For now, though, I was grateful for every second I had with her. And I couldn't wait to see her tonight. It hadn't even been a full day and I missed her like crazy. I was, in every sense, addicted to Rainey. She had so quickly become my whole reason for being. I lived to make her happy.

I stepped out into the hallway to make a call before Luke and Wolfe got up. I wanted to surprise Rainey with something that was sure to make her even happier.

***

When the guys finally woke up, we dragged ourselves out of the hotel and got some breakfast. The diner was a favorite of mine, and I ordered an extra-large cup of coffee.

Luke requested water and toast, his signature hangover meal, and I was amazed by Wolfe's appetite. He ordered eggs, bacon, pancakes, fried potatoes, and a tall glass of milk. Luke almost gagged when the waitress brought us our food.

"How can you eat that much?" I asked Wolfe, who dug in to his meal with fervor.

"What do you mean? This isn't a lot." He frowned.

My eyes went wide. I could put away some food, but even on a sober day I couldn't eat a meal that hearty. And he was claiming it wasn't a lot?

"I'm a growing boy," he mumbled with a pat on his stomach and then washed down a forkful of pancake with milk.

Luke, I noticed, kept his head down and munched on his toast silently. Either he didn't want to hurt Wolfe's feelings or he didn't want to be nauseated by the sheer volume of food Wolfe ate. Once we had all finished, we left a hefty tip for our server and went out to the truck.

"I've got to get a tux," I explained to them.

"Sure. There's a shop downtown that should be able to get you one on short notice," Luke said as he climbed in the driver's seat.

I pulled open the door behind his and jumped in. "Sounds good."

Wolfe grunted his approval from the passenger seat and we were off.

I found a sleek black tux that wouldn't need any alterations. The vest was a faded pink color, which was similar to one of the colors Rainey mentioned she wanted to be our *wedding colors*. If it didn't match the way she wanted, I would just not wear it, I decided. It was in really good shape and the shop didn't want much money for it, so it wouldn't be a huge loss if I had to ditch the vest for the day.

Luke and Wolfe found cheap tuxes that were the same deep black as mine and rented theirs. I could have rented mine, too, but I really wanted to keep the tux as a reminder of my marriage to Rainey. The shop owner suggested they each wear a plain black vest, so they didn't have any conflicting color schemes. He also threw in a white vest and tie for me, just in case the salmon-colored vest didn't work out.

We thanked him and then drove out of Portland to the small town of Casper that I had called home for my entire life. The scenic drive was filled with lots of green from the pine trees and shrubbery. As we came down the hill into downtown Casper, I had to smile at the freshly planted flowers that lined Main Street. It made the town look all the more picturesque and perfect.

My life until that point had been filled with little appreciation for the people and places around me, but as we passed the dozen or so shops, I gave up a silent thanks for everything this town had taught me over the years. Small-town life wasn't for everyone, and I wasn't sure how much I wanted to stay here, but I knew that wherever Rainey wanted to spend her last days, that's where we would be. She had the final say, since she was the one who would eventually be on a deathbed.

When we pulled into the driveway of the house Luke and Mallory shared, the girls were nowhere to be found. I knew they wouldn't be back for a while yet, either. Behind us and right on time, a delivery truck pulled into the drive.

"What's this?" Luke asked, staring at the vehicle with apprehension.

"I ordered something special for Rainey," I explained. I went over to the truck and told the driver what I wanted done in the backyard. He and another guy started unloading dozens of flowers from the truck. "I've got to run over to the hardware store and get a few things. Can you guys supervise the delivery?"

Luke looked at me. "Of course. Where are all these flowers going?"

"Just have them set up around the outer edges of the space. The guys delivering the chairs should be along shortly. We want six chairs on either side of a wide aisle. All the chairs should face the back edge of the yard and leave a space big enough in front of the chairs to accommodate a ten-by-ten alter," I directed them.

"Got it," Wolfe called as he followed one of the delivery guys around to the back of the house.

"Anything else?" Luke asked.

"Yeah, actually. I'm going to need some help to build an arch. It's another surprise for Rainey. You up for the job?"

"You know it." He pounded my outstretched fist and we parted ways.

I jumped in his truck and kicked it in gear, turning out of the driveway and heading toward the hardware store. Rainey wanted a perfect wedding and I was going to make damn sure she got it.

Chapter Twenty-One

Rainey

On the drive back to town, after I'd been thoroughly pampered and beautified, we dropped Ember off at home. She still had several days of school left, and I didn't want her to miss any more days. She would come over Friday night to be at the wedding Saturday.

Mallory's cell rang when we were just a few miles out of Casper.

"Hello?" she answered, balancing the phone between her ear and shoulder as she drove. She glanced warily at me. "Umm, yeah, I can do that. No, it's no problem. I'll see you tonight. Bye." She pressed end and dropped her phone in the cup holder.

"What was that about?" Gabby asked from the backseat.

"Change of plans. We are staying at Wolfe's house now and the guys are staying at my place."

"Why?" I asked, mildly curious.

"I'm not sure. Something about they wanted to make sure things are set up properly or something. Domineering men." She rolled her eyes.

I wasn't exactly thrilled to stay at Wolfe's place, and I was positive Gabby would throw a fit, but to my surprise, she just nodded her agreement and stayed quiet.

I assumed Baker didn't want me to feel overburdened with any of the organizing, so he decided to take over and keep me as stress free as possible. He was so sweet. He gave up a lot of time at work for this wedding, as did all our friends, but I knew how much this week off would cost him.

"So have you guys decided on a honeymoon?" Gabby asked me.

"Umm, not really. We were just in Vegas and I know he won't be able to take much more time off work, so it'll probably be like a night or two somewhere. No big deal," I said.

"Baker has all the time off in the world," Gabby started.

"Gabby!" Mallory chastised her and shook her head at her.

"What do you mean he has all sorts of time off?"

Both of them were silent.

"Tell me now or the wedding is canceled," I threatened, feeling like a total bridezilla and not caring one bit.

"Okay, but don't get mad," Mallory finally relented. "Baker sold the bar."

"He did what? Why wouldn't he tell me?" It was so unlike him to keep something like that from me. I was torn. Part of me was excited that we could be free of the bar for the next several weeks, but the other part of me was upset that he hid it from me.

"I'm not sure. He probably didn't want you to feel guilty, in case you pushed him away again when he went to LA," Gabby suggested.

He sold it before LA? That meant he was even more serious about me than I could fathom. While I was stuck in my own childish tantrum, he had been planning a future for us. And that certainly explained why he had a huge wad of cash in Vegas. As disappointed as I was that he didn't tell me, I decided to see if I could mess with him about it and maybe lure the truth out of him.

I grinned and explained my little plan to the Mallory and Gabby, who wholeheartedly agreed.

By the time we got to Wolfe's house, we were all feeling devious. The guys were all waiting for us and Baker gave me a huge grin as I walked up to him.

"Hey, gorgeous," he greeted me. "I missed you." He enveloped me in his arms and I felt the familiar tingling of contentment in my body, a sure sign that we were doing the right thing.

"Hey, yourself. Did the chairs come?"

"Yep. We've got everything handled," he promised. "Have you decided where we're going to have our rehearsal dinner? I was thinking somewhere local so that we don't have to travel much. I've spent more time lately on the road or in a plane than I have just staying in one spot. I'm tired of being busy."

He gave me the perfect opening. "I have, actually. I figured it would be cost effective to have the rehearsal dinner at The Landing, and it wouldn't cost much, since you're the boss. We could get cheap meals for everyone and then we wouldn't have to empty our pockets for a dinner for our friends," I suggested with a smirk.

Baker had the decency to look horrified. "I don't think that's such a good idea," he started.

"Why not? I think it's perfect. A night on the water will help to relax everyone, too," I explained. "I really want to do it there, Baker."

He sighed. "The thing is, Rainey..." He looked around at our friends who surrounded us, the guys looking sheepish and my girlfriends looking like the cat that ate the canary. "Honestly, the food isn't that good."

Food? The man was a piece of work.

"Well, that's okay," I replied sweetly. "It will just mean a lot to me to have all of us together in *your* bar."

Behind him, Luke coughed and Wolfe averted his eyes. I had Baker right where I wanted him.

"Rainey, I sold the bar!" he blurted, eyes on the grass. When he looked up at me, I had to hide my smile.

"What? Why didn't you tell me?" I gave him my saddest eyes and frown. I tried my best to look hurt.

"I'm so sorry," he began. "I should have. I didn't know how to tell you, though. And then we were in Vegas, and it hardly seemed the appropriate time to say anything. Then the proposal and we were on a plane back here. There hasn't been enough time," he rushed his words together.

I turned away from him and covered my mouth with my hand to stop the giggles that were bubbling up. I couldn't stop my shoulders from shaking, though.

"Rainey! Please don't cry, baby. I'm so sorry." He whipped me around and wrapped me up in his arms so my head was buried in his chest.

I gripped his shirt in my hands, drawing deep breaths to try to stop laughing, but I had a hard time and my breathing was erratic and short. Baker rubbed my back and made *shh* sounds at me in a soothing tone, which only set me off on another round of giggles.

It wasn't until Baker really looked at the people around us that he realized something wasn't right. Wolfe and Luke stood side-by-side, arms folded over their chests a few feet away with huge grins. Mallory and Gabby were on Luke's left, with a hand covering their mouths, but it was obvious they were smiling, too.

Baker gripped my arms and pushed me away from him so he could look at me. "What the hell…?"

I let out my pent-up laughter and gave him a big smile. "Gotcha!"

His hands dropped from my arms and he stared at me, incredulous. "This was a joke?"

"Of course it was! You really think I would be upset about *you* selling *your* bar? I'm not that controlling, Baker."

He finally got over his stupor and shook his head, trying to hide the upturn of his lips. I winked at him and then walked into the house with Mallory and Gabby following close behind. I heard howls of laughter from Luke and Wolfe and the three of them wrestled a bit before they joined us inside.

I sat at Wolfe's dining room table, smiling over the last time I had been here and Wolfe had been encouraging to me.

Gabby sat next to me looking uncomfortable. "So why don't you ask your brother to walk you down the aisle, Rain?"

"Well, he's always so busy and this is completely last minute, so I didn't ask him because I thought it would put some strain on his schedule. I'll ask him to come see me after the wedding, and he can pick the time and not feel rushed or anything."

"There is a bit of a rush, though, isn't there?" Mallory asked from her spot in the kitchen where she leaned against the counter.

"I know..." I searched for the right words to convey how I felt. "I just didn't want to bother him."

"He deserves to know," Gabby said gently as she put a hand on mine.

"He will. I'll tell him," I promised. "I will."

They both seemed appeased about Dallas for the moment and then the guys walked in, interrupting our conversation and covered in dirt from their wrestling session. Mallory got each of them a beer.

Baker walked over to me and put his hand on my shoulder. "So where do you really want to have the rehearsal?"

"Oh, I'm not picky. Anywhere you choose is fine," I said agreeably.

Chapter Twenty-Two

Baker

Friday proved to be a trying day. Rainey's mother called at seven in the morning, refusing to attend the wedding. I felt so bad for Rainey, who was calm and polite on the phone, but obviously stressed out.

"Mom, I'm not going to make you come, but it would be really nice if you did."

"You never even told me about your leukemia. Imagine how I felt, finding out from the gossips in town about it! I've never been more embarrassed in my life!"

Rainey had her phone on speaker, so I could hear every word. I was amazed that her mom could be so selfish and self-centered. Rainey was the one suffering.

"I know, Mom. I should have told you. I'm sorry," she apologized. This was a side of Rainey I'd never seen. She wasn't the feisty woman I knew and loved; she was submissive and quiet. As much as I hated to see her this way, I knew that she had adapted her personality to her mother's, so that she would piss her off with what she said. It was so sad. I wrapped an arm around Rainey's shoulders for support.

When she got off the phone with her mom, Rainey was drained. I suggested she go back to sleep for an hour and then she could be more relaxed for the day. She had finally convinced her mom to come to the wedding, although I wasn't sure it would be a good idea, considering her mom's drug and alcohol problems. Rainey assured me it would be okay and then went back to sleep.

The rehearsal went smoothly and we even managed to convince Rainey to do it outside the restaurant instead of at Mallory's house. I wanted her to be as surprised as possible when she walked down the aisle. We had the dinner at The Roadhouse, a nearby restaurant with a great food selection and plenty of room for the wedding party, not that it was overly large.

I woke up on Saturday with butterflies in my stomach but completely prepared to make Rainey my wife. I would never back down from my decision to marry her, but I was still a little nervous. I slept in the guest room of Mallory and Luke's house and jumped in the shower first thing. When I stepped out of the spray and turned off the water, I heard voices from the kitchen. I put on a pair of khakis and one of my favorite tees and went out to see who was here.

Rainey's older brother, Dallas, was sitting at the table, his hearty laughter nearly infectious. With him at the table were Mallory, Luke, Gabby, Ember and Wolfe, all laughing along with him. I'd seen enough pictures of Dallas to know what he looked like, but he was taller than I imagined, even taller than me.

He stood when he saw me walk in and his smile faded into a serious gaze. He met me in the kitchen, hand extended.

"Dallas Daniels," he introduced himself.

"Chris Baker," I announced. "It's great to finally meet you."

Dallas had grown up with his mother, so I'd hadn't known him when we were kids. When I called him a few days ago, he seemed surprised to hear about Rainey but he took it all in stride, agreeing to come out to the wedding at the last minute.

"Likewise. Word is, Rainey adores you." He nodded his head toward my friends at the table. "And all these people say nothing but good things about you. You're okay in my book, Baker."

I didn't ask for his approval. Hell, ten minutes ago, I didn't even care if I ever got it. But when he said the words, I released a breath I hadn't realized I'd been holding. I might not have asked, but I was grateful for his blessing. I loved his sister, and for the time being, it seemed that was enough.

"Thanks. I'm sure she will be ecstatic that you're here. Speaking of which, where is Rainey?" I asked.

"She asked us to leave the house so she could have some time to relax. The ceremony isn't until seven, so we think she's just enjoying the quiet. Things have been a little crazy around here lately," Mallory replied.

She wasn't wrong. I wished I was able to kick all these people out and have a few minutes to myself. But she was more important, so I put everyone to work.

"We still have to get the lights hung up, so let's get moving," I demanded.

"We have to pick up the flowers in two hours, but we can help until then," Gabby announced.

Once everyone was outside, I started handing out orders. Luke and Wolfe were on lights detail, with Dallas helping as needed. Mallory and Gabby set up the tables for dinner underneath the tent off to the side. It was supposed to rain and I didn't want to take any chances, in case it started to sprinkle during the reception.

White lights were strung up all over the tent to create the perfect ambiance, and then I had them put lights through the arch I built. The arch was threaded with pink and white floral arrangements and each row of white chairs was graced with a pink and white potted plant. It looked amazing so far, even though the lights wouldn't be visible until just before the ceremony.

Instead of a runner down the aisle, we had a basket of flower petals prepared by the florist to be laid down just before the ceremony. Pink and white roses supplied the petals and there were enough to almost fully cover the length of the aisle. Wolfe and Luke would take care of that just before seven.

"I think I'll keep my presence a secret until after the ceremony," Dallas said just before lunch. The girls were about to go pick up flowers, but the three of them stopped.

"No way!" Mallory objected.

"You have to walk her down the aisle," Ember directed.

"I thought she asked Wolfe to do that…?" Dallas looked unsure.

"She did. But only because she didn't want to be a burden to you. I know she would love it if you walked with her," Wolfe said.

"Should I go with you girls, then?"

"No, I like the idea of keeping it a secret, actually. Let's surprise her just before she's supposed to walk down the aisle," I chimed in, knowing how much it would mean to her to have Dallas walk her down the aisle.

With that, the girls took off in Mallory's car and we finished up all the last-minute things for the night. In just a few hours, I would be married to Rainey Daniels.

Correction: *Rainey Baker.*

Chapter Twenty-Three

Rainey

I took calming breaths to slow my rapid heart rate, but it didn't really help.

"Where's Wolfe?" I asked, nerves on fire.

"He's going to meet us there," Mallory promised. "Calm down, girl! Everything is going to be perfect."

It was just after six and Baker had said he was going to send someone to pick us up from Wolfe's house at six o'clock. With the confrontation with my mother yesterday, my nerves were shot. I wanted nothing more than to get drunk, but I knew it was impossible.

"Maybe he forgot. We should just go," I suggested, ready to jump in Mallory's car.

"We'll do no such thing," Gabby admonished. "Baker said he would send someone. He wouldn't lie to you."

Just then, a horn sounded from out front and we all rushed to the windows to see who it was. A white stretch limo awaited us. I blinked away tears, careful not to ruin my makeup. It was perfect.

The driver helped us inside and then drove us to Mallory's house. When I would have gone around the side of the house to start the ceremony, Mallory directed me inside.

"Baker has something prepared for you," she said as an explanation. I raised a brow. "We'll meet you on the other side of the back door in a few minutes. Take your time. We still have half an hour before we have to start." She smiled softly at me and winked.

She took my bouquet and walked around the house to the backyard while I walked forward to go inside. When I opened the door, I was surrounded by darkness, except for a walkway lined with strings of white lights. It was adorable. Five feet from the front door was a photograph hanging from a string. I glanced at it and my heart clenched tight. It was a group photo of my senior prom, the one Baker had taken me to. We looked happy and content. I flipped it over and there was writing on the back.

I think I knew, even then, that I loved you.
~Baker

I sighed with contentment and made my way down the hallway to what used to be Mallory's bedroom. I'd spent so much time there as a kid. I found another photo in her room, hanging from a string, just like the first.

It was a photo from before I ever looked at Baker as more than just the best friend of Mallory's boyfriend. The four of us were sitting on her bed, arms around each other, with Mallory and Luke on the far left, then me, and Baker to the right of me. We all looked so young, so crazed. We each stuck our tongues out at the camera. I'd seen the picture a hundred times in Mallory's room when we were kids, but the longer I stared at it, I noticed something I never had before. Baker's eyes weren't closed like the rest of us. His eyes were wide open and he had them glued to me. They were the same silver pools I knew and loved, but they were dilated, too. I gulped and turned the photo over.

I only ever had eyes for you.
-Baker

I smiled and tried to blink away the tears. Good thing I'd been smart enough to wear waterproof mascara. I heard a door close from somewhere inside the house and ventured out into the hallway again, happy to play this game. It was relaxing me. The hallway had another photo hanging from a string. It hadn't been there a few minutes ago.

I was floored by the image. It was from the night Baker proposed and the couple on the street had taken a few shots of us. Instead of a single image, though, this photo was a collage of all the photos taken that night. I stared at myself and Baker; we looked so happy, so in love. It was the best night of my life to date, and I swallowed the lump in my throat as I flipped it over.

Forever will never be long enough.
~Baker

All the other doors in the hallway were closed, so I moved back toward the living room and into the kitchen. There was a note beside a white rose with dipped pink edges.

Never doubt for a second that I love you. No man has ever been as lucky as I am to find a soul mate so abso-fucking-lutely perfect. And you are. So now, if you're done with your trip down memory lane, could you please come outside so I can marry you?

He didn't sign the last one, but then, he didn't need to. I picked up the rose and inhaled its sweet scent. I heard footsteps behind me and whirled around, certain it would be Baker, anxious to marry me.

I was shocked to find my brother standing there. "Dallas?" I shrieked and ran to him, throwing my arms around his neck. Given that I hadn't wanted to bother him with my illness or wedding, it seemed miraculous that he was there.

His presence made my wedding day complete, my heart full. This was a perfect day now.

His arms went around my waist and he lifted me up and swung me around several times before he set me down.

"What are you doing here?" I demanded, even though it didn't matter.

"Baker called me. I should reprimand you for leaving me out and assuming that I wouldn't drop everything and come to be here on your wedding day…"

"I know. I didn't want to bother you. You're always so busy," I whispered.

"We can talk about it later, baby sis. But for now, let's get you married to Baker. He's one hell of a guy," he commented. He held out his arm for me and I slipped mine through his.

This wedding would be the beginning of the end, but it would be perfect. And I wanted to get it done so I could spend every moment with Baker for however long I had left.

I smiled at my brother, thankful and truly blessed to have him there, and he led me outside.

A million tiny lights lit up the space. It no longer looked like Mallory's backyard. Instead, it was an oasis of perfection. As promised, Mallory was waiting there for us. She handed me my bouquet and winked at me again. She followed Gabby and Ember down the aisle of rose petals, a touch that I knew Baker had been in charge of, and I watched them go, pondering how I got to have such amazing friends. When they took their place on the left side of the alter, my gaze flew to Baker, the man I was about to pledge myself to forever.

He stared at me and a lump formed in my throat. The rest of the world disappeared for one splendid minute and I knew, in that instant, that I was the lucky one in our relationship. And we would probably spend our entire marriage arguing over who was *more* lucky. It was an argument I was looking forward to.

Dallas and I took a step at the same time. His was to give me away to a man who adored me, and mine was a step toward my future.

I lifted my head high, proud to be the future Mrs. Baker.

About the Author

Dawn Pendleton lives in Maine with her husband and their dog. She spends most of her time writing about strong heroines and sexy heroes. When she isn't writing, it's not uncommon to find her with her nose in a book or her eye behind the lens of a camera.

Looking for more from Dawn Pendleton?

The Broken Series
Broken Promises
Broken Dreams
Broken Pieces (release date: December 2013)

The BFF Series
Liar, Liar
Knocked Up
Mall Rats
Terms of Endearment (11/05/13)
Cruel Intentions (11/19/13)
I Love You, Man (12/03/13)
The 22 Year Old Virgin (12/17/13)
Role Models (12/31/13)

Made in the USA
Charleston, SC
11 October 2013